BEST GAY ROMANCE 2011

BEST GAY ROMANCE 2011

EDITED BY
RICHARD LABONTÉ

Published in the United States by Cleis Press Inc.,
2246 Sixth Street, Berkeley, California 94710.

Printed in the United States.
Cover design: Scott Idleman/Blink
Cover photograph: Ocean Photography/Veer
Text design: Frank Wiedemann
Cleis logo art: Juana Alicia
First Edition.
10 9 8 7 6 5 4 3 2 1

ISBN: 978-1-57344-428-6

...still romancing
the Asa

Contents

INTRODUCTION: IT'S FOR THE HEART TO HOLD FAST

Sometimes romance lasts a languorous lifetime; sometimes it's realized in a singular, startling moment; sometimes it's a wish that remains unfulfilled; sometimes it endures after death. So many want it in their lives; so many fear asking for it. It's often the province of the young, but witnessing romantic elders can be transcendent. Sometimes it's a flirtation nestled within a relationship, sometimes it's prelude to a friendship, and sometimes it's an emotional bonding unrealized—a romance *manqué*.

Romance embraces a multitude of experiences. As does *Best Gay Romance 2011*.

Eric Nguyen's story of high school boys on the cusp of manhood is about confronting uncertainty. Anthony McDonald's story of youngsters meeting again as men is about shucking expectations. Derrick Della Giorgia's story of a well-born man and a butcher's son is about overcoming barriers. David May's story of a leader wooing a lesser-born—but not a lesser man—is about negotiating differences. David Holly's story about love in collision with hate is about standing up to homophobia. Martin Delacroix's story of one man exulting in a summer romance and another man clinging to the closet is about the release of self-liberation. Jay Mandal's story of love blossoming after a bashing is about besting trauma. In each story, there's the possibility of happy-ever-after—the warm, beating heart of romantic desire. (And Simon Sheppard's story of two lovers meeting again after a separation heralds romance in the hereafter....)

Not every desire to love through a lifetime is realized: Tom Mendicino's story of a chance encounter at Christmas is about evolving through passion into friendship. Jameson Currier's story of a mediated encounter at a dinner party is about two paths not quite crossing. Tyler Keevil's story of a college football player's attraction to a literary aesthete is about gentle rejection. Shanna Germain's story of a young man's attraction to an older man and the role his own father plays in that longing, is about... well, that would be a spoiler. And Edward Moreno's story of sex on the side respects how a relationship can be flexible.

So: romance is not a one-size-fits-all proposition. It encompasses a spectrum of possibilities, an infinity of beginnings, middles and ends. Whether fleeting or forever, it's for the heart to hold fast. Read all about it here.

Richard Labonté
Bowen Island, British Columbia

ONE FUNERAL AND…

Anthony McDonald

I was just three when I first went to Endes. It's one of the earliest memories I can reliably date, because of the five-hour train journey from London to Scotland and the fact that it snowed hard all the way up: new experiences both and guaranteed to make an impression on a small child. Uncle Max met us at Dumfries station—at the wheel of his vintage Rolls-Royce, which was another thing a three-year-old wasn't going to forget in a hurry. Nineteen years later, I can still bring to my mind the smell of its leather seats, as clear and sharp as if they were with me now, though the car is long gone.

The rest of that visit is less clear, details overlaid by memories of another one four years later. But I remember my wonder at the sheer size of the house, a major culture shock after our own modest home in North London. And the breakfasts: Jenny softly banging the brass gong to summon everyone; then Uncle Max at one end of the long, highly polished table and Auntie Annie (who was my mother's first cousin and the only reason for our being invited to Endes at all) at the other. Uncle Max ate differently from the rest of us: grapefruit halves, then Ryvita crispbread instead of toast. He was on a *die-it*, whatever that might be. For the rest of us it was the Full Monty: bacon and eggs with mushrooms and tomato, or grilled Finnan haddock, even for me. I'm ashamed to admit I remember the food that Jenny served us more clearly than I remembered the other people who sat around the table with us: that is, the three children of Uncle Max and Auntie Annie—my second cousins. Isabel and Marie were a few years older than me and to my eyes seemed nearly grown up. Both had flaming red hair. Their little brother Felix made less of an impression, though he was the same age as I was. His hair was almost black, not fiery red, and he was—the adults all said—*shy*. I remember that instead of giving you a clear view of his eyes when you looked at him, he showed you a pair of long dark lashes. No doubt we played together in the wintry garden and the big old house, but I don't remember that.

We did play together four years later, even if a bit reluctantly. This second visit to Endes took place in early summer, and even my seven-year-old self was conscious of the beauty of the Scottish lowlands then, washed alternately, almost minute by minute, by warm sun and short sparkling showers: a countryside of emerald and diamond. The girls were now fourteen and twelve, far beyond the games of their little brother and myself, so the two of us were thrown together for the week by default. I can't say we clicked. I thought the seven-year-old Felix was stuck-up, snooty, conceited, pompous and cold: all those adjectives (even if they were not all in my vocabulary at the time) that we use to pigeonhole those people by whom we are subconsciously, and usually unnecessarily, intimidated. (I know now, of course, that Felix felt exactly the same, back then, about me.) He didn't speak with any suggestion of a Scottish accent; rather he had the posh and assured tones of a boy who has been put down for Eton and knows it. (He didn't go to Eton, in fact; he went to Fettes, which is approximately a Scottish equivalent—the school, incidentally, attended a generation earlier by one Tony Blair.) I'd thought *we* were fairly posh, and me especially, even though there was no way I'd be going to Eton. But Felix's degree of posh unnerved me, put me on the back foot, and so, when our week in Scotland came to an end and I left feeling I would miss so many things—the countryside, the walks with the gamekeepers and the dogs, the breakfasts, the arrival in the kitchen of whole fresh salmon from the River Nith—the company of Felix was not included in the list.

A couple of years later Auntie Annie died, of cancer, at the wastefully early age of thirty-eight. I remember that my parents traveled up for the funeral, though I didn't; I was away at boarding school. And after that there were no more visits to Endes. My parents and Uncle Max exchanged cards at Christmas, but that was all. When I was about fifteen he remarried. His new wife—somewhat improbably in the wilds of Galloway—was a woman from Argentina, called—hardly less improbably—Lolli.

In the middle of last summer, the phone rang. It was my parents' phone, but I was living with them at the time and, because I happened to be in that afternoon and they out, I answered. It could have been—would most usually have been—the other way round, so it was just chance. Chance! What a maligned word, *chance*. How we undervalue it. Since that day, that moment, I have given a super-healthy respect to Chance.

The voice on the phone was unfamiliar, but once the name was given I knew exactly who it was. I hadn't met many other people called Felix. He was phoning to say—and would I pass the message on to my parents—that his father, Uncle Max, had died. Quite suddenly, unexpectedly, but without pain or fuss. I made the usual polite noises, condolences. If there was anything any of us could do... Please let us know when the funeral was to be, and we'd make every effort to be there if we could. On an impulse, though perhaps it was just a reflex born of habit, I gave him the number of my mobile phone.

"I don't think they'll expect us to go all that way, you know," my mother said, when I'd passed the message on. "Of course I'll phone young Felix and speak to him myself, but I don't think anyone really expects... This woman...Lolli...the second wife of a cousin's husband, and we've never met. And the children... Well, okay, they're your second cousins, but even so..."

"Well, I think I ought to go," I said and heard myself sounding a bit over the top as I said it. "As a representative of the family, you know. On behalf of all of us. Show some support for Felix." My mother looked at me oddly, as well she might. Felix had done very well for the last fourteen years without my support, or even any contact between us, and I'd managed very nicely without him too. My mother had never heard me mention his name, and I'd scarcely given him a thought.

But I wasn't quite as mad as I must have sounded. I was living at home, aged twenty-one, having graduated from university in the middle of the biggest recession even my parents could remember, with no job to go to and no prospect of one. I was doing some part-time work for the Royal Mail, on special deliveries. Real fun? I'll leave you to guess. It wasn't surprising that I'd want to grab at the chance to get out from under my parent's feet with a trip to Scotland. Even so, my parents might still have talked me out of it quite easily. (Simply not offering to pay my train fare might have been enough.) But then, less than half an hour later, I received quite a long text from Felix.

He actually spelled in full the words *could use some support.*

No, he didn't expect a full state visit from my family. But if by any chance... Chance...

And as soon as I liked.

I told my parents what Felix had said. I would take the sleeper that evening... The sleeper? Cost a bloody bomb...! Well, all right then, the overnight train. Sit up all night. Neck-ache in the morning. Arrive red eyed... My father gave in and let me use his credit card to book a sleeper-berth online.

Felix met me at Dumfries. Not in a Rolls-Royce but in a respectably mud-spattered Range Rover. It was six in the morning, so his presence was good of him. It gave me a shock to see him get out of the car and, with a question in his voice, call my name. "Jonty?" The shock was that he had grown beautiful. He hadn't been at age three or age seven, from what I could remember, but then I'd hardly have been on the lookout for male good looks in those days. Or I don't think I was. But now my immediate thought, the cheap, base one, which you've guessed already, was...*Is he gay?* Not, I wonder how he's coping, what he's feeling, losing his second and final parent at twenty-one. None of that. Simply: *Is he gay?* How quickly the thought springs to mind when we meet a new person that we fancy. How much longer before we ask ourselves that question when it's someone that we don't.

For all the northern fairness of his skin he had a look more common in South America than among Scots. It was as if he'd inherited them, against all the laws of nature, from his Argentinian stepmother, Lolli, rather than from his real mother, my Auntie Anne. His eyes were large and liquid brown, his eyelashes dark and long. His eyebrows were beautifully shaped, very dark too, as was his hair, which was curly and thick, but longer than most gay guys our age would choose. He was about an inch less than me in height (I'm five foot ten) and very slim. Though that didn't make him particularly small, he had a delicacy of build—being small boned and finely made—that rendered him both attractively petite and, paradoxically, slightly better muscled than he was. In the same way, though his shoulders were not especially broad, they appeared so in contrast to his slender waist and narrow hips. How he might look from behind I'd have to wait to see. His voice was beautiful too, and he spoke, these days, with a very light Scots accent.

So, was he gay? I hadn't even thought to think the question till I saw him. Now it preoccupied me, though there was nothing in his manner to suggest he was. We greeted each other with open smiles and a cousinly but perfunctory hug, then got into the car, but there was nothing in my manner to show that I was either, as I'd discovered long before now. Even my parents had been disinclined to believe it when I first told them, though in the end they were—thank heaven—very nice about it.

As we drove along, the warmth generated by our encounter and greeting dissipated somewhat. I think this was because the reality of our situation was beginning to strike home. I'd traveled four hundred miles on a whim, a whim that was joint property of myself and Felix, to spend time with a cousin I hardly knew, at a particularly delicate and difficult moment in his life and that of his immediate family. Now that I was actually here—and with the funeral itself still five days away—I was suddenly awkward, unsure about what I was here for, what I was supposed to do.

Before going to sleep in my bunk the previous night *(For you dream you are crossing the Channel and tossing about in a steamer from Harwich, which is something between a large bathing-machine and a very small second-class carriage,* as Gilbert and Sullivan put it) I had found myself trying to picture Endes in the throes of full mourning, but laziness and incipient sleep had given me only the scene in *Four Weddings and a Funeral* where Andie MacDowell marries a dour but wealthy older man in a Scottish baronial castle, and a kilt-wearing Simon Callow dies of a heart attack after dancing the Highland Fling. I'd been just awake enough to tell myself there wouldn't be dancing. I wasn't going to even one wedding but to a funeral, full stop.

The same uncertainty about what was to be done with me now he'd dragged me all this way must have struck Felix at the same moment as it did me. Trying to make small talk as we drove through the Galloway countryside (emerald and diamond again in the bright morning) I could feel us slipping back, becoming again the stiff, self-conscious and prickly selves we'd shown each other that last time, when we were seven. I didn't know what I wanted in the way of a rapport between us now, but I knew I didn't want that. I took the bull by the horns. "What do you actually want me to do, now I'm here?"

It sounded really awful. Like I couldn't have been ruder if I'd tried. I added, in a rush to make amends, "I mean, I'm here to help out in any way I can. Just tell me what you want. I'm at your service."

Felix had looked startled at my first question—which was fair enough—and had taken his eyes off the road for a second to look straight at me, but then, as he heard my attempt to explain myself, there came a quick smile before he returned his gaze to the road ahead and he said, "You know, I hadn't really thought. I think I just wanted you to be here. If that doesn't sound too stupid to say to someone I hardly know." A hint of awkwardness clouded his voice.

"We've known each other nearly twenty years," I said, wanting to ease his sudden discomfort. He would know my answer for the silly, fatuous one it was, but would recognize, I hoped, the friendly spirit behind it. The look of his last quick smile was still etched behind my eyes. He had full lips and a cute, pert nose. His smile had made his brown eyes sparkle and transformed him for a moment into a slightly larger than average pixie.

He said, "It was nice the way you spoke when you answered the phone yesterday. I'd had a whole day of phoning cousins. But you sounded different. Sorry. Forgive me. I'm a bit emotional at the moment."

"It's okay," I said, wondering why he'd thought he had to apologize. It wasn't as if he was tearing up or anything. There'd been no crack or tremor in his voice. But of course it was okay if he felt emotional. He'd lost his father just forty-eight hours earlier, an experience I'd not yet had and didn't know how I'd deal with when I did.

Then suddenly, there it was. That moment of vulnerability, the crack in the armor of his invincible beauty, had done it for me. We hadn't yet asked what we did for a living, if we were still students; neither yet knew even if the other was married, for god's sake. But it was at that moment, as he turned into the long driveway, beneath the tall trees where herons precariously nested—as I suddenly remembered—that I fell for him. I had fallen for him—to mangle metaphors most horribly, but somehow no other one will do—hook, line and sinker.

Endes looked exactly the same. The gong, though silent this breakfast time, was still in the morning room; Jenny, now elderly and plump, was still in the kitchen, to welcome me with a matronly hug. Dogs greeted me as before, though inevitably not the same dogs. Formality was gone, though, especially this week that stretched awkwardly between death and funeral rite. Breakfast was not a sit-down affair today, but a casual do-it-yourself in the kitchen, like breakfast in any other busy house. Felix, though he had a hundred and one things on his mind, made sure I got fed, that I was introduced to everyone who came and went—especially to his stepmother and his two red-haired sisters and their husbands—and he showed me to my room. "It's the one you had last time," he said. It surprised me that he remembered. I hadn't. Perhaps all junior ranking guests were put in that room and had always been.

Doubts about my usefulness, questions about what I was going to do, quickly melted away. Felix had to drive into Kirkcudbright to see the funeral directors and chase up the death certificate, over which there'd been some admin confusion or delay. Lolli was due to go to a meeting with a solicitor in Dalbeattie, which was in the opposite direction. She shouldn't have to go alone. Would I...? Of course. Could I drive her car? Did I actually...? Yes, of course I could drive. Of course I would. If Lolli would direct me as we went along.

To my surprise I remembered the way into Dalbeattie from all those years before and didn't need to be told. My passenger, dressed in smart but sober gray and white was (I was not surprised by this) surprisingly young. Uncle Max had been seventy, but his widow looked to be on the right side of thirty-five. Felix's sisters, I'd noticed, treated her as an honorary elder sister.

So, your wealthy elderly husband's dead, you're a good-looking South American, footloose in Scotland. What's your next move? There are some people who would actually say that. I'm not one of those people. I'm with the rest of the world—who'd just think it. And, despite the fact that we were on our way to see a lawyer, and presumably that very question was going to be discussed behind doors that would be closed to me, she didn't volunteer any information on the subject. Instead, she talked about Felix.

He was midway through his studies at medical school in Glasgow, where he shared a flat with other medics. In my brief conversations with him so far this morning I hadn't got as far as finding that out. When you go to family gatherings and meet distant cousins in their parents' homes you often make the lazy assumption that that's where they live. Of course they rarely do. Just because I was living with my parents at age twenty-one didn't mean that Felix also was. The other thing that Lolli told me was that Felix had a girlfriend called Rhona, daughter of another prominent local family, whom he was expected to marry.

I met Rhona a couple of hours later. She came to lunch. She sat very prettily next to Felix at the table and was charming when she talked to me. Soon after lunch she left. I was alone with Felix for a brief spell after that. He showed me round the house, not all of which I'd seen as a child. If I say there were eight bedrooms upstairs, and attic rooms above that, that gives some idea of how big a place Endes was. "Rhona's very nice," was all I managed to say about his girlfriend. "Oh, yes, she is," he answered, and smiled. We were in the snooker room at the time and, as he spoke, Felix picked up a cue and neatly pocketed a stray ball, as if to show beyond argument that that particular avenue of conversation was closed.

Rhona didn't appear for dinner, though some elderly neighbors did, a Mrs. MacComb and a couple called McClerg. Felix's sister Isabel was there, without her husband. She and Marie were taking it in turns to stay over, night on night off, and be company for Lolli. I thought that very good of them, though obviously it wouldn't go on forever. Some time after dinner was ended a moment was reached when the guests had gone and Lolli and Isabel had retired to their rooms, as some people still say, and Felix and I were suddenly left alone. I was about to say, out of politeness (and shyness also), that I would "retire" too, but Felix, probably sensing this, jumped in very quickly with,

"Do you want a whisky? We could take it out on the terrace."

There was nothing I'd have liked better. Well, there was, but with Felix practically engaged to Rhona that didn't seem an alternative realistically to be hoped for. "Laphroaig do you?" Felix asked. One of those smoky, peaty single malts that taste like burnt toast crumbs—a flavor I don't much care for. I said it would be perfect.

We sat out in the long northern midsummer dusk, and while light lasted in the sky, and the rolling hills and woods went gray, we talked. I told Felix I'd just completed my degree in English but what did you do with that? He understood: he had friends in Glasgow and Edinburgh in the same position. I told him I was working as a postman. He laughed and said, so were they. I learned about Felix, his studies in Glasgow, his life there... I found we had interests in common, opinions and tastes we shared. I dared to think that our personalities were a little bit alike. I told him, rather shyly, that I wanted to be a writer. He said, "If I knew you a bit better I'd ask to read something you wrote." Everything he said, everything he was, I liked. He was a wonderful new discovery, and I couldn't get enough of him. We didn't discuss sex. With someone who's going to be married and who you've only known as an adult for a dozen hours...well, you don't. Only after several whiskies (I take back what I said about Laphroaig: it's brilliant stuff) was I bold enough to say, "About this place." I gestured to the house behind us and waved vaguely across the lawns in front of us, and the darkening landscape beyond. "What happens to it now?"

"It's mine," he said. "All mine. Every brick and stone. Every wood and field and pond. Every cottage on the estate." He didn't sound at all happy about this. "And I'm just trying to become a doctor."

"But your sisters?" I said. "And Lolli?"

"Lolli gets a house on the estate to live in rent free for life—if that's what she wants to do."

"And you get the big house?" I should have worked this out for myself but I hadn't. I was slightly gobsmacked. "It sounds more like 1910 than 2010," I said, which was not very diplomatic of me. When whisky talks it rarely counsels prudence. But Felix didn't take it badly. He laughed and said, "It may be 2010 in London. Even Glasgow..." and left it there. "My sisters," he went on, "each got a packet when they got married. A very generous one. They don't come in for any more."

"You mean, like a dowry?" I said. It sounded medieval.

"No, Jonty," Felix answered, the use of my name making me feel like a reprimanded schoolboy. "The money remains theirs; it wasn't handed over to their husbands. We may not have joined the twenty-first century but we've got beyond the Middle Ages."

"Sorry, Felix," I said. He topped up my glass.

"The thing is," he said, sounding like this thing was rather a big thing, "it's all in the expectation of my getting married. Marrying Rhona. Who as well as being stunning looking and intelligent is pretty wealthy in her own right."

Mind your mouth, I told myself. *Don't let the whisky say anything*. "Hmm," I said, and asked about the agenda for the morning.

It did get dark eventually and we went inside. "Will Rhona be over tomorrow?" I asked then, as we washed up our glasses in the kitchen rather than leave them in the dishwasher for Jenny to deal with in the morning.

"No," he said. "She won't be over again till the funeral. She lives in Edinburgh. Her own flat in the New Town."

Edinburgh. I was astonished by that. A pretty long drive from Glasgow, an even longer one from here. I'd drunk two large whiskies since I thought we didn't know each other well enough to talk about sex. I said, "Do you...I mean...do you sleep together?"

Felix looked suddenly awkward and for a moment I saw him as a three-year-old again as his eyes hid themselves behind his long lashes. "No, we don't."

To spare him I looked up at the kitchen clock. It said one o'clock. "Hey," I said. "I can't believe that's the time." I'd been awake since four, watching the dawn on the fells and the Scottish border, and Felix must have woken early himself to come and meet me off the train at six. "I guess it's bedtime." We said good night at the top of the stairs and went our different ways along the landing.

The next day was another round of errands and tasks that kept Felix and me in separate orbits for most of the time. I drove where I was told to, delivering and collecting things and people as required. You don't realize how much there is to do when someone dies, until you find yourself in the thick of it. It was after dinner, nightcap time, before Felix and I were alone together. I'd spent all day looking forward to this moment: stupid, lovelorn me. And yet when the moment came, there was a look of something in Felix's eyes—soon to be married Felix, didn't sleep with his girlfriend Felix—that made me wonder, though not too hopefully, might he have been looking forward to this moment too?

We took our glasses—and for good measure the bottle too—out through the French windows and onto the lawn. There was some special stuff you had to burn (Felix had used it the night before too) to keep the midges away. We said, "Cheers," to each other, clinked glasses, then Felix, sitting beside me on the grass, turned his whole body toward me, looked me full in the face—his own face looking very serious, troubled even—and said, "I'm gay."

There followed an echoing silence, like in a cavern. It was as if Felix had heaved a boulder over the edge of something and was waiting for the splash. I realized that he was waiting for me to speak. I said, "So am I." It wasn't the moment to tell him I'd been in love with him for forty hours.

He really did, quite literally, sigh with relief. "I didn't know you were," he said very quietly. "I really didn't. You don't show it in any obvious way..."

"Neither do you..."

"...But I kind of hoped it. Since I heard your voice answer your parents' phone the other day. You were so...friendly. I mean, I know that doesn't mean a person's gay. I mean... Oh, shit, I'm sounding stupid."

Not half as stupid as I wanted to sound, blurting "I love you" into his face. I had almost physically to restrain myself. "It doesn't sound stupid," I told him instead. "It sounds...nice."

Two guys tell each other they're gay. It doesn't mean they want to sleep together, let alone that they're going to. I mean, imagine it in a hetero context. He: "I'm straight." She: "Me too." See what I mean? Doesn't get you very far. I took a sip of whisky to give my racing thoughts time to catch up. "What about Rhona?" I asked eventually. "Does she know?"

He shook his head, his face tense with worry again. "No. No one does."

I could understand him being reticent with his very traditional family. "But your friends in Glasgow," I said. "You must be out to them?"

"Only one or two. Not with most of them."

"But are you...?" I didn't know how to put this. Did he have sex with anyone? Had he ever?

"Do I have a busy sex life, you mean. No. Except for the obvious. Though I've done enough to know what and who I am. But that's it."

I decided not to pursue this further. But he did, with me. "What about you?"

"I had a couple of affairs at uni," I said. "Nothing major. And I don't have anyone now." Actually I'd had more than a couple of affairs at university, but I wasn't going to rub his nose in it. And the last part was true at least. I hadn't had sex with anyone for months.

Now it was I who'd pushed something over the precipice, and it was his turn to react. But he took his time, gazing away through the dusk toward the distant fields, which all belonged to him. Then he looked back at me, his eyes haunted and big, like dark lamps. He said, "Can I kiss you?"

We went to his room that night. It was farther away from the others' than mine. Stripped naked, he was more beautiful than ever, more beautiful than anyone I'd slept with or even seen. To my surprise, and probably to his, neither of us had much of a hard-on. We were too awed, I think, by the situation, by whatever (we didn't dare to name it aloud) had happened to us. We simply stood facing each other, next to his bed, taking in each other's naked, glowing form. I reached out a hand and ran it down the middle of his chest to just above his navel, where a tiny central line of hair licked up from below like a slender black flame. He began, silently, to cry.

He had every right to, I thought. The stress of losing a father and now this. But by what right did I then follow his example and into the silence spill a load of tears myself? I took him in my arms and he took me in his.

No other kind of load was spilled by either of us that night.

We cuddled ourselves to sleep. But first light found us both with robust hard dicks, and we each came, with almost comical superabundance, in the other's hand, overflowing our bellies and soaking the sheet, before I reluctantly tiptoed from his room and back to mine.

For the next two days we led a double life. We spent our nights together, in the full flood of new love, and we spent our days pretending that we didn't, pretending that we weren't. In the evenings we couldn't wait for the others to go to bed. Our whisky intake was reduced (good for our livers) to a single glass, and that was downed in record-breaking time, so impatient were we for bed, for the other's body, the other's dick. For the whole, wonderful, wondrous other person. Felix for his Jonty. Jonty for his Felix.

After a couple of days—we were in the garden at the time—Felix said, "Stay on a few more days after the funeral. Please. Phone your parents. Tell the Post Office you need a few more days off."

"The Royal Mail," I said. "They're not the same thing anymore."

"Whatever," Felix said. "I don't want this to end. It can't."

That was how I felt too. But I said, "It can't go on forever. You know it can't. I can't live under your roof indefinitely and nobody twig. Think about Rhona. Unless you intend to tell her and have the whole thing out."

"I *want* you here indefinitely," he said crossly. I'd never known him other than mild tempered in the four days since our idyll began, though he was cross with himself more than with me. Then he stamped away across the lawn.

I didn't attempt to follow him. *I want that too, I want that more than anything*. But I said the words to myself.

I didn't think we'd have to wait till the funeral before seeing Rhona again, and I was right. She came for lunch that day and stayed most of the afternoon. She was friendly toward me as before, and we talked easily over the lunch table, but I let Felix be alone with her in the afternoon, finding jobs for myself to do, taking the dogs for a run. After she'd gone, Felix said to me, "I've told her you'll be in the front row with us in the church tomorrow. You and me with Lolli and Rhona on one side, my sisters and their husbands on the other."

I thought this an odd way to proceed. It fell right between what I'd thought of as the only two alternatives—to go on clandestinely as we were until our affair petered out, or for Felix to make a clean breast of it and let his house fall about his ears. For I was quite sure that if he did come out to Rhona and his family, his sisters and Lolli would be able to challenge his father's will and kick him out of Endes for good. Then what would happen to him and me? Would we share a small room at my parents'? Both of us work part time delivering letters? Or would I go to the Glasgow flat and be unemployed and in the way there? I couldn't see our fragile, new-hatched love surviving either of those eventualities. I couldn't see anything that didn't look like a dead end, a brick wall. I guessed the same went for him. "How did she react to that?" I asked.

"She was fine with it," was all he said.

We didn't discuss Rhona or any of this again that day. Neither of us was able to. We waited till night came and then took refuge in each other, in sex. We were good for that, at least. Felix had had his first fucks with me, on the giving and receiving end just half an hour apart, on our third night. He was a gentle lover and a wonderful one. When he first entered me he made sure we were face-to-face. He wanted to see the blue light of my eyes, he said. He said they were like the sky. Often we were happy enough to pleasure each other by hand, to enjoy the sight of our milk-white spurts and our bellies aflood. His cock was not enormous and neither were his balls. But they were the most beautiful I'd ever seen, his cock elegantly hooded, which mine (he laughingly compared it to a shillelagh) is not. He also called me beautiful, which stunned me. Other people had done, once or twice before, when they'd had a certain amount of drink inside them, but none of those had Felix's looks: that face, that perfect body. I wouldn't have imagined for a moment that I might appear beautiful in Felix's eyes, but apparently I did. That night before we buried his late dad we hugged each other closely, with little hope for the future beyond the next few days.

The service went like clockwork. Felix was a meticulous planner, his sisters too, and I'd helped. The little church in Dalbeattie was packed, and bright with sun; the showers held off. When the coffin was carried in, a swallow followed through the open door and flew quickly round the church before returning to the outdoors. I heard Lolli whisper to Felix that it was his father's soul, freed now to fly through the sunshine. Caterers came to Endes to prepare food and drink. A huge number of people came back from the church to eat and drink it. And though you're not supposed to notice this, the quality of the provisions was seriously good. Felix looked outrageously handsome, formally attired and in a kilt. He looked terrifically sexy in it, those handsome legs of his, which I knew so well the feel of, on public show; those well-formed, perfect calves. I wondered, watching him, what everyone always wonders about kilt-wearing Scotsmen and couldn't wait for the opportunity—which I knew wouldn't come before nightcap time—to find out. (I did find out at nightcap time, out on the lawn. I ran my hand up the soft inside of his warm thighs and found no barrier between my fingers and his businesslike cock and balls. He was already very wet up there in anticipation, and hardening at my approach, and my exploring hand was shortly replaced in that warm darkness by my head. But I'm running on a bit too fast.)

Rhona came looking for me among the crowds that drank to Max's memory that afternoon. She was dressed in brilliant black. I was nervous of her now but could hardly run away. "It was nice to have you with us in the church," she said. "I mean at Felix's side." I must have gaped at her, because she smiled and said, "Sorry. I know that sounded really silly. Those things are. But today it mattered. You see, I know it mattered, because I know what it means."

"You know what it means?" I blustered. "What does it mean?"

She put a hand on my arm, very gently. "You know what it means." She stopped a moment. "Sorry. These things are difficult. What is expected of us. Who we are. They don't always fit. Jonty, you don't need to look at me like that." (I didn't know how I was looking at her. I tried to smile. It felt a bit flinty.) "Felix is a very sensitive boy. You know that, of course, because so are you." She paused a half second. Then, "I know that Felix is gay. We've been friends since childhood, and I know him very well. I guessed some time ago."

"You're all set to marry him," I protested.

"Don't be hard on me for that," she said. "I thought we could make a go of it, Felix and me. We could be platonic, even, if he preferred it that way. We're very, very fond of each other, you see. It might have worked. For many people, even these days, it still does. But then I met you. I thought, four days ago, or five, whenever it was, seeing you with Felix... It was nothing the two of you did, or said to each other. But I kind of knew. I told myself I'd imagined it. Then yesterday... Well, yesterday the truth was just too clear. I know you scarcely exchanged a glance all lunchtime, being considerate, I suppose, to me. But when you did...the static filled the air. I was glad he told me about wanting you at the front of the church with us...I mean, with him. It'll be easier for him now when he's ready to tell me the rest."

My thoughts were a maelstrom. "You're going to marry him," I said. What I meant by that, exactly, I don't know.

"No," she said. "Not now. It's you he loves. He doesn't need to say it. It's just so. You love him too." I was too stunned to speak. She said, "I'll leave you in peace now," and walked away.

We hadn't used the word love to each other, Felix and I. Not up to that time. God knew, we'd both wanted to, but we were scared of it. To say "I love you" is a very daring thing. But that changed that evening, as everything changed that evening, out on the lawn, once I'd freed my head from the embraces of his kilt.

We continued our lovemaking in his bed. Getting away with a blow job on the lawn when we were both fairly fully clothed was one thing but, though no one had ever come out, or peered through a window at us, during our nightly garden whisky talks, we thought that stripping naked out there might be a bit foolhardy. And there were always the midges to be reckoned with. Safely tucked up, we both came more times that night than we'd done in the nights before, Felix spurting deep inside me, me emptying myself into him. Felix joined to Jonty, Jonty joined to Felix. The words *I love you* came from Felix, came from Jonty, and came and came again.

Nearly a year has passed. The countryside is wearing its diamond and emerald spring look again.

I went back to my parents' a week after the funeral but only to collect my belongings. I never delivered another package for the Royal Mail. But if I ever thought that managing a big estate was easy work, well, I don't think that now. It's incredibly tough, and you have to get up...well it doesn't bear thinking about how early. But if Felix is here for the night he has to get up early too. He goes off to Glasgow, by car to Dumfries and then by train. (It takes forever.) And if he's not here for the night, then I'm with him in his rather narrow bed at the Glasgow student flat. I'm not going to go on and write more paragraphs about how beautiful he is, how good sex is with him; about his gorgeous cock and the sweetness of his character and disposition. You can reread the descriptions of him I wrote earlier if you want to and change the tense to the present as you go along.

We see quite a bit of Rhona—and her new man, Callum, who's a hunk. They're good friends of ours. As for Lolli, she didn't take advantage of the rent-free house in the grounds in the end. She's also found a boyfriend—if you can call anyone of fifty that. They're in London most of the time. But when they come to Scotland they stay with us at Endes. We've eight bedrooms, after all.

On the rare occasions when I'm not with Felix, and I'm not working hard around the estate, negotiating with tenants, replacing fence posts or whatever, then I write. And Felix, when he comes back, however tired he may be after a long shift on the wards, will read what I have written and, if I'm lucky, approve.

LIBERTY! FRATERNITY! SEXUALITY!

Tyler Keevil

He was one of the last to arrive, drifting through the door like a leaf or scrap of paper. I don't know why he made such an impression on me. It wasn't like there was a shortage of girls in that writing class. Some of them were hot, too. But beautiful girls were common in my life—I picked them up at frat parties every weekend. This was different. I'd never seen a beautiful guy before. He reminded me of a river dryad: shocking blue eyes, curling blond hair, delicately shaped throat. I stared at that throat, and those eyes, until our teacher arrived.

"Hello, everybody."

She was a hoary-headed woman with small breasts and big hips. Taking her seat at the head of the table, she scattered a mess of books and pens and notepaper in front of her.

"Why don't we introduce ourselves?"

It was just like preschool. We took turns, going around the room.

"My name's Kim. I'm majoring in English lit..."

"Hi. I'm Sakine. I just finished *The Incredible Lightness of Being...*"

There were six women in the class, the teacher, and us. He looked completely at ease, but I was in agony. I didn't want to introduce myself. I hated that kind of thing.

"Hey," I said. "I, uh, play tight end on the varsity football team."

Polite nods were the only response. I dropped my eyes. The room seemed to have shrunk so that the walls were squeezing my sides, the roof pressing down on my shoulders. I was the big, stupid jock—too big and stupid to fit in the class. I sat, flushed and hot faced, and missed the next few introductions.

Then it was his turn.

"I'm Tad," he said. He had a high, sweet voice. It wasn't masculine, but it wasn't quite feminine, either. "I'm studying English." He paused, looking thoughtful. "I've never written anything before, but I'd like to start."

He flashed a shy smile. Everybody smiled back, accepting him. Why couldn't I have said something like that, something open and honest and real? For the remainder of the class, as the teacher ran us through some writing exercises, I found myself sneaking surreptitious glances in Tad's direction. I couldn't help it. It was the way he moved, I think, even when he sat still. His gestures were languid and natural, like a free-flowing mountain stream.

I was more like a hunk of rock.

Saturday nights we partied.

A bunch of us from the football squad would get decked out in our team jackets and crash the nearest frat party. We'd pay our five bucks and guzzle beer, then hit on sorority girls in hopes of getting laid. Successful nights ended in drunken sex back at our dorms. A night of failure meant slinking home and jerking off to piles of well-thumbed pornography.

"All the chicks look the same to me these days," I said.

I stood with Kevin, our quarterback, to one side of the makeshift dance floor. A glistening disco ball threw colored leopard spots over frantically wiggling bodies. None of us ever danced. We stood drinking our beer from plastic cups, peering at female shapes through a haze reeking of perfume, sweat and testosterone.

"You need to experiment," Kevin said. "You can't stick to meat and potatoes."

"I've tried a lot of stuff. It's not that."

"You tried hoovering?"

"No, I haven't tried hoovering."

"You should." He burped under his breath and blew it out the side of his mouth. "A good hoover makes any lay worthwhile."

We both shut up as a blonde appeared on our radar. She was a classic sorority clone: fake and bake tan, caked layers of makeup, cleavage spilling from a low-cut top. I was vaguely aware that there were other women in the world, real women, but I was convinced they all lived in Europe or Quebec City. Until I got there, my options seemed limited. The blonde strutted past us, then glanced back at Kevin and flashed a pornographic smile.

"She's up for it," he said.

He ran a hand through his hair, freshening the spikes. The gesture was identical to the one he used before we broke from huddle, when we were preparing to run an important play.

"Look," he said, slapping me on the back. "Have a few more drinks and go find Sarah, huh? She's been begging to fuck you again. I'll see you at practice tomorrow."

I watched him go after the blonde. She didn't put up much of a fight. Pretty soon they were grinding away and sucking on each other's face. I knew I'd have similar luck if I could muster Kevin's enthusiasm. Sarah was around somewhere. I felt a vague twinge of excitement in my abdomen as I imagined being hot and naked and sweating with her. Then I thought of the sticky aftermath: the dwindling erection and the oily condom full of frustrated semen, and the hideous attempts at small talk. I wasn't drunk enough to make the leap into absurdity. I chucked my beer, still half-full, into the garbage and wandered back to my dorm. I flipped through an old copy of *Penthouse* I'd been given for my nineteenth birthday, lazily eyeballing the familiar contours of two-dimensional female flesh. Nothing doing. I couldn't even get wood. Instead I got out my notebook. I was supposed to hand in my first story on Monday. I didn't have a story. I didn't have an outline. I didn't even have an idea.

I was already beginning to regret joining the class.

I got into the class on the strength of one story, about a child losing his father. I wrote it about my own father, without knowing how or what I was writing. My teacher kept encouraging me to write something similar, something that would help me find my voice. But I didn't want to find my voice or talk about my father with all these strangers. Instead I handed in bizarre tales about distant planets, as far removed from my own life as possible.

The first story I handed in was a disaster.

"This language is so archaic!"

"I don't even know what it's about."

"Honestly, I couldn't finish it. I'm sorry, but I just couldn't."

I sat, tense and uncertain, while they ridiculed me.

Then somebody said, "I enjoyed it."

Everyone shut up. I was as shocked as the rest of them by

the notion that my story might be likeable. I was even more surprised when I realized who'd spoken. Tad was looking out the window, in a distant and dreamy way, at the rain-wet trees and murky gray skies.

"There's some rough parts, but it's a neat idea." He waved his hand, as if trying to pluck the essence of my story from the air. It was about a kid who plugged himself into a video game and never came out. "It's very Ray Bradbury." He fixed me with his blue, unblinking eyes. The rest of the class seemed to recede. "Have you read 'The Veldt'?"

I nodded eagerly. "That's where I got the idea."

A rustling of papers ruined the moment. "Yes," the teacher said. "Genre fiction can be interesting, but next time you'd do best to hand in something with a more personal slant."

She had to put her negative seal on the discussion, but I was used to that. I barely listened. I smiled stupidly. I was so grateful that somebody had understood my story, understood me. I wanted to reach out and shake his hand. No, I wanted to hug him. Then I wanted to sit him down and talk. He had told me my story was neat.

It was the nicest thing anybody had said about my writing.

I was even more aware of Tad after that.

I looked forward to each class, looked forward to seeing him and hearing him say pleasant things about my stories. I always returned the favor. That wasn't hard. Everybody loved Tad's stories. He wrote wild, freewheeling flights of fancy. He wrote about pigs with wings and the farmers that raised them. He wrote about a limbless midget who enjoyed being tossed down bowling alleys, about women who made love to corpses and about a boy whose face was one enormous zit. In that class, where everybody else composed painful confessionals about sex, relationships or dying relatives, reading one of Tad's stories was like suddenly emerging into open air after hours of hacking your way through dense jungle.

I wanted to write like that.

Our class lasted for two hours on Tuesday mornings, from ten until noon. I kept hoping that somebody would suggest we all go out for lunch. Then I'd have an icebreaker, an excuse to hang out with Tad. But nobody ever did. If I was going to meet him, I'd have to take the initiative. It wasn't a big deal—I just wanted to talk to the guy. But with Tad it *seemed* like a big deal. Each class, I got all jittery whenever the opportunity to speak with him arose: at the water fountain, in the toilets, by the photocopy machine where we duplicated our manuscripts. I hated it. It got to the point where I couldn't sleep, or eat or do anything.

I was terrified I'd never get to know him.

After class one day the teacher took me aside. She had my most recent opus in her hands: a thirty-page epic detailing the exploits of futuristic assassins. It had gone down in class like a skydiver without a ripcord. Whatever she wanted to talk about couldn't be good.

She said, "I don't feel like you've accomplished anything this term."

I waited, arms crossed, biting my lip like a baby.

"Everybody else is developing a voice. You keep writing genre fiction."

"Maybe my voice is genre fiction," I suggested.

She glanced at the first page, then rolled my manuscript into a baton so she could gesture with it while she spoke. "You need to write about something that matters to you. Then it will matter to us. If things don't change, I'll be forced to fail you on your portfolio."

She offered me the baton and left the room. I held the manuscript as it unfurled like a dove that had died in my arms. Maybe she was right. I was a football player, not a writer. I was still standing like that when Tad came back, flowing along in his nonchalant way. Seeing me, he smiled demurely and explained, "I forgot my pen."

There was a pen on the table beside me. I handed it to him automatically.

"Is everything all right?" he asked.

I didn't say anything. I clutched my manuscript.

"Come on," he said. "Let's get some lunch."

We went to the Dugout Bistro on campus. It was as dark and intimate as a cellar; there were no windows and no natural lighting. Tad ordered a green salad with almonds and fresh lemon. I watched him squeeze the lemon between his delicate fingers, nursing it for every last drop of juice. His nails were painted white and turquoise, like exotic bits of shell. All I ordered was beer. Between nervous gulps, I picked at my napkin, tearing off little pieces.

"Are my stories really that bad?" I asked.

Tad put down his fork and said, "No."

"She says she's going to fail me. I can't afford to have that on my transcript." By this point my napkin was in tatters. I pushed the scraps around, arranging them like pieces of a jigsaw puzzle. "I should never have joined a writing class in the first place."

"Why did you join?" He leaned forward, propping his chin up with the heel of his palm, and treated me to his shy smile. "Aside from obvious masochistic tendencies, I mean."

"I needed an arts credit."

"Most of the jocks take psychology or communications courses."

He had a point. Kevin had already slept with half the girls in the psych department.

"I guess I wanted something else," I said. I shrugged, staring down at my hands. The fingers looked thick and awkward. "I mean, I'm sick of football and partying. I wanted to try something new. Writing seemed adventurous. That must sound pretty lame, huh?"

Tad shook his head. "It doesn't sound lame at all."

Our server appeared, tray propped on one hand. She had the look that usually caught my eye: compact figure, full mouth, natural hair. As she cleared Tad's dishes I sized her up without much enthusiasm, as if my libido was running on autopilot. She pointed to my glass.

"You want another one of those?"

I glanced at Tad. I wasn't sure how much time he had to spare.

"Oh, go ahead. Come to think of it, bring me a vodka seven, too."

I smiled gratefully. While we waited for our drinks, he told me about the story he was working on: a postmodern fable about an animal rights activist who married his pet panther, then got mauled on their honeymoon. Like everything else he'd written, it was genius. I listened attentively, gazing into his soothing blue eyes as his words washed over me. The rest of the bistro faded slowly into soft focus, like the background in a film.

Lunch at the Dugout became our secret ritual—one that counteracted the weekly torture sessions I endured at the hands of my classmates. Each workshop, they hacked me up and spread my innards all over the table. Then they took their time picking over the spoils.

"You can't take it so personally," Tad told me.

But I did. I wanted to stand up for myself, only I didn't know the words. I sat in agony as they shredded my work. Then I'd gather together my insides and scuttle over to the Dugout with Tad. The beers helped; listening to him helped even more. His words were like a cooling balm over my fresh wounds. Magic words.

"Just imagine if they all tried playing football."

"I'd slaughter them. I'd face-mask them and slam them to the ground."

I smashed my fist on the table to demonstrate. I was pretty drunk at the time.

"Exactly. They'd give up after one practice, after one play. You've already got that on them, right?" He smiled. "Besides, do you really care what somebody like Kim thinks?"

I laughed, choking on my beer.

"No," I said. "I guess not."

Kim was a spiteful girl, a mean girl. She had large breasts that she hid beneath thick woolen jumpers, even on painfully hot days. This made her sweat. She hated my stories. Everybody hated my stories, but she hated them most of all. She sat in class sweating and hating and waiting to make known her hate. She usually spearheaded the attacks against me.

Our next class was no different.

"I can't believe how simple this story is," she said, rolling her eyes. "There's no depth or complexity to your style. You write like a child who's just learned the alphabet."

Usually I wilted beneath her criticism, but Tad had empowered me.

"I know you hate my style," I said, glaring at her. "That's all you ever say. I hate how you write, too—it's totally pretentious—but I don't keep bringing it up all the time."

Silence. A bit of backbone was the last thing they expected from me.

Then Tad said, "He's got a point."

I smiled at him, my knight in shining armor.

I loved hanging out with my knight, but there were drawbacks. He drove guys crazy, for one thing. They always came up to him—when we were in the bistro, or the cafeteria or walking to class. Some of them knew him and some of them wanted to know him. It made no difference to me. I hated them. They were so obviously queer. They batted their eyes at him and made those limp-wristed gestures, telling him bullshit stories about their little gay lives. They always ignored me. I bristled with palpable animosity, like a homophobic porcupine. I especially hated one guy who kept turning up. He looked like a "Baywatch" reject: tall and darkly handsome, with watery, inflated muscles and a little girl's voice.

"Hey, Tad, honey. Are you going out this weekend?"

He'd cornered us in the cafeteria. I wanted to throw my salad in his face.

"Maybe. What about you?'

"I'm going down to Celebrities with a bunch of the boys. You should come."

"I'll think about it."

"You do that. See you, honey."

I stared after the guy, jaw tense. Tad couldn't help but notice.

"Are you okay?"

"What?" I asked, acting innocent. "Oh, sure. Fine. What were we talking about?"

"My new story."

"I haven't read it yet," I lied.

I stabbed at my salad, deliberately ignoring him.

* * *

Football practice started halfway through term.

With Tad on my mind, it was hard to concentrate. As a tight end, my job was to crush people. I would run and smash into them. I rammed my helmet into ribs and kidneys. I dove and took out knees with a forearm or a shoulder. I tackled high and low and finished each game aching, exhausted, satisfied. I loved the physicality of it. I loved the skull-rattling, bone-jarring impact of body against body. But my fixation with Tad made me wonder if that love covered up another love. Did I only like football because I liked grunting and heaving and sweating amongst packs of guys? Was I out there involved in some great, grassy orgy, fumbling for the ball like a virgin for the right hole?

I had to find out.

I started peeking at the guys in the showers, trying to discover if I was gay. Amongst the smell of man-sweat and hot steam, I studied the smooth, athletic asses and the various-sized cocks, from slender and long to thick and stubby. Some of the guys had balls like dangling chestnuts, others had tight little acorns. But I'd seen it all before, and none of it interested me—my own dick never even quivered. I was safe. I wasn't gay. At least, not in the strictly physical sense of the word. I didn't want men in general. I only wanted Tad.

Sarah spotted us one day while we were sitting in the Dugout.

"Hey, babe!" she called, wiggling her fingers.

I forced a smile to my lips as she came over. She looked good. That was nothing new. Sarah always looked good. She dressed like most of the sorority girls: short skirt, squeaky new runners and a snug T-shirt with the usual brand-name logo across the front.

All that was fine—I'd never had a problem with her appearance.

"I haven't seen you for ages," she said, tousling my hair. "You avoiding me, babe?"

"Just busy."

"I know, don't you hate school?" She pulled up a chair, raking it across the floor, and settled into it, making a big show of adjusting her top. Then she looked at Tad. "Hi!"

I introduced them.

"You'll never guess what happened to me today..."

We listened to Sarah tell inane stories about arguments in her carpool, about flirting with her English professor, about the terrible tempura she'd had for lunch. She talked and talked without saying anything. It was painful and a little embarrassing. After about ten minutes Tad politely mentioned he had a class to get to and stood up.

"See you next week," he said.

Sarah and I watched him stroll away, lean and unflappable in his hip-hugging jeans and tight navy shirt: a little boy blue outfit. With his blond hair, he looked great in blue.

"I love gay guys," Sarah said. "They're so sexy. How'd you meet him?"

"He's in my writing class."

She wrinkled her nose, as if she smelled something funny.

"You? Writing? You're kidding, right?"

I sighed. "No."

"I mean, like, what do you write about?"

"I don't know. Stuff."

I didn't want to tell her, and she didn't really want to hear about it.

"So," I asked her, "you going to Kevin's party next weekend?"

"I can't wait! It's going to be so much fun."

That set her off. She loved talking about drinking and partying. I listened, nodding in all the right places, but apparently it wasn't enough to fool her.

"Wait a minute—you're coming, right?"

"I don't know..."

"Oh, you have to come." She put on a pouty face and shimmied a little, drawing attention to her breasts. "I mean, if you don't come then who will I go home with?"

It was a good question.

"All right, man!" Kevin screamed. "You made it!"

He grabbed me in a bear hug and held me off the ground. Lights and noise assaulted me from all sides. Kevin lived a few blocks off campus, in rented accommodations he shared with three other guys from the team. Most of our crew was there, a bunch of frat guys and dozens of sorority girls. Across the room, clusters of nervous freshmen were gathered like tadpoles around the keg, waiting their turn. Everything was exactly as I remembered.

I felt nauseous.

"Man, I'm so glad you showed," Kevin shouted over the music, one arm draped drunkenly across my shoulders. "You hardly ever come out anymore. What's up with that?"

"Aw, shit, I'm super busy these days."

"You sniffing any pussy?"

"Not much. You?"

"Always, man. Always."

I knew I needed to start drinking, and quickly.

"Where you guys hiding the booze in this shit show?"

"That's my boy!" He yanked me close in a playful headlock. "Come on—we'll get you started with a keg stand. Later we'll haze a few of these freshmen faggots."

Kevin loved bullying freshmen, probably because he'd gotten it so bad himself. He shoved a bunch of them aside, clearing our way to the keg, then stuffed the hose in my mouth and started working the pump. I sucked the beer back like a man dying of dehydration. Once I got going I couldn't be stopped. I wanted more and more. I wanted to blot out the image of blond hair and mesmerizing blue eyes that haunted my days and nights. I blasted it with beer, bombarded it with vodka shooters, battered it with rum and coke. It almost worked. I got drunk enough to convince myself I was a man, virile and ready to fuck like a man.

That was when Sarah found me.

"What do I spy with my little eye?"

She rubbed up against me, leering and breathing gin fumes. I didn't resist. Somehow we stumbled our way up the stairs and into a room and out of our clothes. I clutched and squeezed and groped her, savoring the feel of hot female flesh, desperate to convince myself I still wanted it. All my wild-eyed pounding managed to fool Sarah, but it didn't fool me.

I knew who I was really fucking.

There were dull echoes in my skull, like tiny hammer blows. They got louder and louder. Eventually they pounded me to awareness. I groaned and rolled over, squinting through sticky eyelids to get my bearings. Somebody was banging on the door from outside.

"Hey—open up, man!"

"Fuck off."

"That's my room!"

Dirty gray light seeped in through the window, oozing across Sarah's pasty body. A puddle of puke was pooled on the pillow between us. I didn't know whose it was, but the reek of sweat and sex and vomit nauseated me. I started retching and dry heaving.

"I'm gonna break this door down!"

"Just a second. Christ."

I stumbled to the window, fumbled with the latch, and opened it just as a bitter rush of acid, beer and vodka exploded from my throat. It spattered onto the back porch, bright and pink like strawberry juice. I felt better. I grabbed the puke-stained pillow and tossed it out the window. Then I lurched to the door and opened it.

"It's about goddamned time!"

"Sorry, man."

I shouldered passed Kevin's roommate. I had to get out of there.

"Hey—what about your girl?"

I leered at him, swaying on my feet. "She's all yours."

I staggered the half-dozen blocks toward campus, leaving puddles of vomit in my wake. My throat burned, my head throbbed, my arms trembled like a palsy victim's. I convinced myself that I was dying. Tad would never know how I felt about him. In some ways it was a mixed blessing. Nobody else would ever know, either. I'd die a straight man.

I thought: *Yes, let me die. I want to die. If I don't die, I'll have to tell him. I'll have to approach him and ask him out.* I didn't want to do that. What if he said no? What if he said yes? It was terrible. Terrible. I couldn't take it. I crawled into my room and into bed, a vampire tormented by the light of day. *Yes, let me die. Now, I will die. Now. Now. Now.*

Unfortunately, I didn't die.

"The writing is just so, so beautiful."

"Some parts made me cry."

"I loved it. It's perfect."

Listening to the others compliment Tad's story, I felt like a steel spike had been driven through my skull, right along my spine, nailing me to the chair. It was as if he'd written it just for me, filling it with unrequited love, gay sex, homoeroticism, repression.

Then it was my turn.

"I, uh, really liked it."

A circle of unblinking eyes floated in front of me, waiting.

"There are some really vivid scenes."

"Like what?" the teacher urged.

"The sex." My cheeks started burning. I shifted in my seat. "The sex is really vivid."

"Oh, yes, the sex!"

Everybody loved the sex. They began discussing it. I sat back, sweating and exhausted, as if I'd just given birth. We analyzed the intricacies of Tad's writing for the next half hour. I tried to say as little as possible, nodding and agreeing loudly to give the illusion of enthusiastically partaking in a discussion that actually left me vulnerable and exposed, like an overturned starfish.

After class, as usual, we went to the Dugout.

"You didn't like it," Tad said.

It was the last thing I expected him to say.

"No, no—I did."

He laughed. "I know you well enough to tell when you're lying."

"I'm not. I swear. I liked it a lot. It's just..."

"What?"

Finally, I looked up. I took a breath.

"It hit a little too close to home."

His eyes went wide, filled with understanding.

"Oh."

I put down my beer glass. It was already empty. I'd gone this far. I'd walked up to the edge of the cliff. Now it was time to throw myself off.

"I was thinking," I said slowly, trying not to mumble, "I was thinking that maybe sometime we could, you know, go out for a drink or something, something more than hanging out here. If you wanted to."

I was fumbling, falling, looking to him for a lifeline. He took his time, his expression distant and thoughtful. He knew what it meant, knew what it meant to me. Then he smiled.

"You know, I'd like that."

I started breathing again. The beer was buzzing in my brain and suddenly I felt light, lighter than air. I wasn't falling. Tad had been waiting right there to catch me all along.

We arranged to meet up on the weekend, at an off-campus bar in Kitsilano called Nirvana. Tad wasn't there when I arrived. I'd only seen the place from the outside. It catered to Westside yuppies and older students: low lighting, funky décor, candles on every table, chilled-out music, open mic Thursdays. I ordered one whisky, drained it at the bar, then took another with me to a corner table. I huddled there, tense and uncertain, for about a quarter of an hour. By the time Tad turned up, I was totally wired on nerves and booze.

"Hi," he said, slipping into the chair opposite me. He was wearing what he always wore—sleek jeans and a loose, button-up shirt—and he was drinking what he always drank—vodka seven. "I've only been here once or twice. What do you think?"

"It's great," I said, a little too loudly. "I love it."

I looked around: at the other patrons, at the resident DJ, at anybody but Tad. I couldn't sit still. I couldn't shut up, either.

I babbled on about inanities, sucking desperately at my drink, trying and failing to sound even remotely relaxed. At one point, in the midst of my frenzy, Tad reached over and squeezed my hand. The sudden contact startled me.

"It's okay," he said, waiting for me to meet his eyes. "We're just two friends out for drinks. It doesn't have to be any more than that."

His touch was like a grounding wire. I could breathe again. I focused on that while Tad talked, calming me with his word-magic and his steady, hypnotic gaze. He talked about average things, everyday things, things that put me at ease: books and writing and stories.

"Are you working on anything?" he asked.

I nodded. "I don't know if it's any good."

"Science fiction?"

"No. Something different. Something new."

He held up his glass, a casual toast.

"New is good."

As the place filled up, the DJ switched from jazz to funk. There was a small space in front of his booth that had been cleared for dancing. A couple of girls moved out to groove. The noise level rose a few decibels as voices and laughter competed with the music.

Tad drained his vodka and stood up.

"Do you want to dance?" he asked.

"I can't dance."

"You can't or you don't?"

"I can't. It's a genetic defect. It's pretty weird, actually."

He laughed and left me, sliding onto the dance floor to join the girls, wriggling his hips with expert ease. He danced like he wrote: carefree and uninhibited. It was as if he was the only one out there, as if nobody was watching. I wanted to dance like that, to move like that, to write like that, to be like that. Why couldn't I? What was stopping me?

"Dude!" A hand clamped my shoulder. "What's up, man?"

Kevin. I blinked at him, as if he'd just woken me up.

"Hey, man," I said. "What are you doing here?"

"What do you think? Sniffing pussy." He jerked his thumb toward the bar. "Me and a bunch of the boys thought we'd go hunting fresh meat. Who you here with, anyway?"

"My buddy, Tad."

I gestured, helplessly, towards the slim figure shimmying on the dance floor.

Kevin snorted. "He looks like a fag."

I didn't say anything. Kevin looked at me, frowning.

"He isn't, is he?"

"What?"

"A fag."

"Oh, I don't know."

Noticing our scrutiny, Tad detached himself from the girls and sashayed over. I sat rigidly in my chair, gripping the armrests like a passenger on a plane going down, down, down. I knew there was nothing I could do. Sooner or later the plane was going to crash.

I introduced them.

"Hi," Tad said, offering his hand.

It was impossible to miss the freshly painted nails. Kevin looked like he'd been slapped. He glanced from me to Tad and back to me. Then he quickly grabbed Tad's hand, touching it like he was fearful of infections, and, muttering some excuse, retreated to the bar.

"Who is that guy?" Tad asked.

"Our quarterback."

"Oh."

I was all too aware of Kevin and the others, whispering and staring in our direction.

I said, "There might be trouble."

"Maybe I should go."

He looked to me for an answer. I was tempted. It would be so much easier.

"No," I said finally. "Let's see this through."

He smiled. "In that case, I'm going to get a drink."

"I better go with you."

I followed him, ready to run the gauntlet. A wall of bodies blocked our way.

"Hey, guys," I said with forced cheerfulness. "You want a round?"

Kevin crossed his arms, stepping between me and the bar.

"Who's buying? You or your boyfriend?"

The others snickered. I stopped smiling.

"He's not my boyfriend."

"That's what it looks like to me." He poked me in the chest with his forefinger, sticking his face close to mine. His breath smelled of beer and garlic, and I could see hairs poking out of his nostrils. "You better come clean, man. Are you a faggot or what?"

He was like a big, hairless ape, backed up by half a dozen other apes. At one time I'd been an ape, too. Now I was above them, looking down. A flying ape. Super-ape.

"Maybe I am, Kevin." I said. I felt strangely calm. "Does it really matter?"

"Yeah, it fucking matters!"

"Why?"

"It just does, okay?" He grabbed Tad by the collar, jerking him forward. "Now tell it to me straight. You owe me that much, at least. Are you fucking this queer? Huh?"

"What if I was? Would you beat the shit out of him?"

Kevin hesitated. Our little altercation was attracting attention. People had quieted down to watch. Kevin glanced around. He hadn't expected to be drawn into a debate.

"Let him go, Kevin," I said. "What's wrong with you?"

"What's wrong with *me*? I'm not the fag here, okay?"

"Are you sure? Christ—you're so fucking homophobic it's insane."

"Don't call me—"

"You've been homophobic ever since the seniors stuck that broomstick up your ass at our hazing."

"You're a goddamn liar!" he screamed.

He let go of Tad and charged me. I wrapped him up and we went over a table together. Beer bottles shattered on the floor. He was hitting me, so I hit him back. We rolled around in a cold puddle of beer and glass shards, grunting and swearing. Eventually fatigue set in. I stopped punching him and just sort of held him, with one arm looped around his neck. Kevin hit me a few more times in the ribs, weak and feeble blows I barely felt. Then he gave up, too. We clung to each other like exhausted lovers. I could feel him trembling in my arms. I thought of all the stories I had in me, ready to write.

"It's okay, man," I whispered. "It's okay."

Eventually the guys separated us.

Later, Tad and I walked down to Kits pub. It was a clear night, moonless and magic. The cold, stabbing air left an iron taste in my lungs. Fall was over. Not even the leaves remained. Everything was fresh and bare, swept clean. We split a beer while we walked.

"Was that true—about the broomstick?"

"Yeah," I said.

"That's messed up."

"I got off easy. They shaved my balls and threw a bucket of piss on me. I've always hated that shit." I took a deep breath through my nose. "I get sick just thinking about it."

"Which is why you're hanging out with a faggot."

I laughed. "Exactly."

We walked in silence for a few minutes.

Then Tad said, "Your new story. What's it about?"

"Wait and see. You'll like it. The class will hate it, but you'll like it."

There was a line-up at the pub. We huddled in the cold behind two girls in skirts and heels. One of them wasn't much, but the other looked good. My eyes instinctively roamed along her calves to the hem of her skirt, just above her knee, then up to the hips and waist and shoulders. When I glanced at Tad, I saw that he was watching me and smiling in that way of his. Like he knew something I didn't. I shrugged and held up my hands. Helpless.

"I make a terrible gay."

"I know," he said. "But let's pretend you haven't figured that out yet."

Stepping forward, he tucked a finger under my chin, tilted my head up and leaned in to kiss me. His lips were firm and cool and moist. Then he drew back. I blinked at him, my mouth tingling from the contact.

"Something to remember me by," he said.

The line moved forward, and we followed the girls inside.

PILLION

Jay Mandal

I was in the wrong place at the wrong time—my own fault. So I had taken my beating in silence. This was just another gay bashing.

Afterward, blood and tears streaming down my face, I cried like a little kid.

Someone was coming.

I stopped crying and held my breath.

The footsteps drew nearer. It was one of the yobs from earlier, come to finish me off. *Oh, god.*

"You all right?"

"Fuck you care."

He smiled. "You're brave, I'll give you that."

"More like stupid. Just get it over with." I closed my eyes.

When I opened them again, I found he'd crouched beside me and was wiping my face with his handkerchief.

"It's not very clean," he said, "but it'll have to do. Can you walk?"

"I think so."

"Do you think you could ride a motorbike?"

"What kind of question's that?"

"Pillion. My bike's just around the corner."

We stared at the 250cc machine. I could barely walk, and goodness knew what injuries I had sustained.

"I've got a better idea. Wait here." He ran across the road to the all-night café and went in. A couple of minutes later, he came out, followed by a middle-aged man.

"Christ! You never said he was in this state!" the man complained.

"There's a five pound tip in it for you."

The man thought for a moment. "I'll get a rug from the trunk. I'm not having him mess up my cab. He's not going to be sick, is he?" He glanced over at me.

I shook my head. Not a good idea.

They got me into the taxi and then shut the door.

"I'll follow you on my bike," my attacker said.

"I'm not falling for that one," said the cabbie. "Money upfront."

"Thanks," I said to the driver as he pulled away. "I was beaten up, in case you're wondering. There were three of them. I didn't stand a chance."

"I don't want to know."

It was midweek, and Accident and Emergency was quieter than usual, and I was soon examined.

"How is he?" my assailant asked, as the nurse was cleaning me up.

"Mostly superficial. Looks worse than it is. He'll need to see his own doctor, though. Are you taking him home?"

"I'll see that he's looked after."

The nurse drew the curtains on her way out of the cubicle.

"I can't go home like this," I said. "My parents will have a fit."

"I'm not taking you home. You're coming back with me."

"If you think I'm going anywhere with you—"

"Don't worry, I know just the place. Trust me."

And, for some reason, I did.

"Whose flat is this?"

We'd taken another taxi, my companion saying he'd return later for his bike.

"It's mine to all intents and purposes."

"Yours?" It certainly didn't look like the sort of place someone like him would own.

"My grandmother gave it to me. She made me promise not to tell my father."

"Why?"

"She thought it might come in handy."

"No, I meant why aren't you allowed to tell your father?"

"She said he was a philanderer. He'd use this for all his trysts. She hated the way he treated my mother."

"So she was your mother's mother?"

"My father's. Just didn't like her own son. Blamed it on *his* father."

"Why did she get married, then?"

"It was practically an arranged marriage. In some ways it worked. He turned a blind eye to her activities."

"She had lovers, then? Wasn't that hypocritical?"

"Just the one. He was an artist. They used to come here. She would sit for him—perfectly respectable paintings most of the time—and then they'd make love."

"'Most of the time?'"

"There were nude studies, too, but they were never put on public display. He died of cancer in the seventies. She never got over it. He was the love of her life."

"She sounds fascinating. I'd like to have been able to meet her."

"Maybe you will."

"I thought she was dead?"

"Hardly. She lives in the south of France with a young man." His face registered concern. "Are you all right? You look as if you're about to pass out."

"I'm just a bit tired."

"The bed's through here." He led the way. "I can't offer you much in the way of refreshment. I'll have to do some shopping if we're going to stay here. But there's orange juice and biscuits."

"Any water?"

"Yes, of course. I'll get some."

But I was asleep before he returned.

When I woke up, everything ached: my head, my ribs, my back. I could barely open my eyes. Whether that was the result of my bruises or the bright sunlight streaming in through the window was difficult to say.

I looked for my watch. It wasn't on my wrist or on the bedside table. That was when I realized I was naked. He must have undressed me. I hoped that was all he had done.

There was a glass of water on the table next to me. I winced as I leaned over to reach it. My mouth was dry and tasted of blood.

I sat up slowly, and wondered where my host was. Not in bed with me, for which I was grateful. The flat was quiet, so maybe he was still asleep or had gone to collect his bike. I should seize the opportunity and leave.

There was a mirror in one corner of the room. I managed to get out of bed and stagger over to it. The sight I saw wasn't pretty. Cuts and livid blue and red bruises covered my body and face. I needed a long soak in a hot bath to ease the aches and pains and wash away the smell of fear. It came rushing back to me: the alley, the shouts, the kicks, the taste of vomit and dirt.

I froze. I could see his reflection in the mirror. *How long had he been in the room?* "Don't you knock?" I said angrily, grabbing the bedclothes to cover my nakedness.

"In my own home?" he said, eyebrows raised. "How are you?"

"I'll live."

"Good. I've been out to get some food."

"I'm not hungry," I lied.

"I'll put everything in the fridge—it'll keep for later."

When he'd left the room, I looked for my jeans. They weren't there. *Sod it*, I thought, and went to find him.

"What have you done with them?" I demanded. "My clothes—where are they?"

"They're in the bathroom."

I stared at him as if he were speaking a foreign language.

"I washed them. They were filthy."

Maybe I should have been grateful, but I wasn't. "So I'm supposed to walk the streets naked, am I?"

"You don't have to walk the streets"—a pause—"naked. I'll find you something of mine to wear." He began to rummage through the wardrobe.

"First, I need the bathroom."

"I'll have to move your clothes. They're hanging over the bath to dry."

"I need to take a piss, not have a bath."

"It's this way."

I looked for a lock, but there wasn't one. Was there no privacy in this place?

My clothes hung neatly on a stand over the bath. I could be dressed and out of there in a few minutes. I grabbed my shirt, but it was still damp. My jeans had scarcely dried at all. I'd be adding pneumonia to my list of ailments if I went out in them.

"Are you okay in there?" came a voice from outside the bathroom.

I washed my hands, then opened the door.

"I was afraid you'd passed out again. Most of my stuff is round at my parents' house, but I think there'll be something you can put on, at least until your own things are dry."

He got out a shirt and a pair of trousers, which he laid on the bed.

I stared pointedly at him.

"I'll make a start on breakfast." He left the room.

I pulled on the trousers. They were on the big side, but that was better than too tight. As I shrugged into the shirt and did up the buttons, I could smell bacon frying. God, I was hungry, but I wasn't ready to admit it. I contemplated staying in the bedroom but thought he'd only come looking for me.

I found him cooking breakfast. I couldn't see any cuts or bruises on his hands.

He glanced up, and smiled. "Are you sure you won't have some? There's plenty here."

"I don't think I'm up to it yet." I hoped he could hear my words above the rumbling of my stomach. "Where's my watch?"

He put down the spatula he was using to turn the food and went over to the windowsill. "Here." He held the watch out to me. "It was covered in blood and dirt. I got the worst off."

Soon, breakfast was ready. He dished up, sat down opposite me and began to eat. I could hardly bear to look.

"I'll collect my bike when I've finished this." He cut a tomato in two, and put one half in his mouth. "Are you always this quiet?"

"Only when I've been beaten up." I gazed, mesmerized, as he speared a sausage. "What happened after I passed out?"

"I put you to bed."

"Is that all?"

"What d'you mean?"

"Where did you sleep?"

"In the armchair."

"Couldn't have been very comfortable."

"I've dossed down in worse places."

"Your conscience didn't keep you awake, then?"

He paused, then said slowly: "I never touched you last night." He picked up the last piece of fried bread, and held it out to me. "Are you certain I can't tempt you?"

I shook my head and then coughed loudly as my stomach complained about the lack of food.

"Are you all right?"

"I'm fine."

He finished the bread, pushed back his chair and stood up. "I'll get my bike now. Will you be okay on your own?"

"I daresay I'll find something to keep me occupied."

"There's always the washing-up." He collected his keys, wallet and crash helmet and left.

The flat was quiet once he'd gone. I decided to investigate my surroundings.

There were several pictures on the walls of a woman in her late twenties or early thirties. Her face was more arresting than strictly beautiful, with clear blue eyes and a flawless complexion. She seemed familiar. Then I realized: she and my host had the same coloring and bone structure.

The shelves held an eclectic mix of books. There were some on art, others on architecture and even one or two about classic cars and motorcycles. There was a small section containing works by Wilde, Forster and others whose names I didn't recognize. I took one out at random. It was a gay novel translated from the French. *Pip* was written inside the cover. So now I knew the biker's name.

Although I'd known he was joking, a stubborn pride made me attempt the washing-up. My hunger pangs increased as I rinsed grease off the plate and scraped tomato skins and bacon rind into the bin. Pip had put the leftovers in the fridge. God, I was *so* hungry. I couldn't resist it. I helped myself to some scrambled egg and bacon.

Despite my swollen lips, it was the best thing I'd eaten in ages. I put the plate back in the fridge.

Just in time: I heard the key turn in the lock.

"I'm back," Pip called.

I didn't reply.

He put his keys on the table and then took off his crash helmet. The similarity to the woman in the paintings was remarkable. "Would you like some tea? Or do you prefer coffee?" he asked.

"Tea, please," I said before I could stop myself.

"I hope you've made yourself at home."

"Don't think I'm staying."

"You can't go home in your present state. You need time to recover—you can barely move." More gently, he went on: "You've had a rough time."

"You should know. You and your friends half killed me."

"They're not my friends."

"You didn't object when they began kicking the crap out of me."

"That's something I'll have to live with for the rest of my life."

"I'm going home."

"Your clothes aren't dry."

"Put them in a bag. I'll send yours back to you." I swayed and had to put out a hand to steady myself.

"Come on, Adam, you should be resting." He came round to my side of the table and helped me back to the bedroom.

"How d'you know my name?" I asked.

"I noticed it when I took your wallet out of your jeans to wash them."

"Helped yourself to the cash in it, did you?"

"I'm no thief."

"Just a thug." I collapsed on the bed. "I know your name, too. It's Pip."

I slept for several hours. It must have been late afternoon by the time I surfaced. Next time I'd leave the washing-up. My body still ached, and there could be no more ignoring the fact that I was ravenous. Then I heard the sound of a softly played flute: beguiling, beautiful and somehow haunting. I closed my eyes. Eventually the piece drew to an end, and the more prosaic sounds of crockery and cutlery took its place.

I found Pip in the kitchen.

"Good sleep?" he asked.

I nodded.

"This'll be ready in half an hour. You must be starving. No wonder you nearly fainted."

"We need to get some things straight."

His lips twitched at the last word.

"I'm being serious." I glared at him.

"You're beautiful when you're angry."

We stood facing each other.

"Adam," he murmured.

I held my breath.

Then he took a step forward. Our eyes locked. To my dismay, I realized I had an erection. Worse, I knew Pip was aware of it, too.

I expected him to say something flippant, then I realized he was waiting for me to speak. I remained silent.

Unexpectedly, his eyes softened. Another step, and I could feel his breath on my face. His lips brushed my cheeks. "Oh, Adam!" he whispered, nuzzling my hair. He kissed my neck.

My hard-on grew even stiffer. He moved closer, and his hands gripped my buttocks.

"Ouch!"

Pip looked comical in his surprise.

"I had a kicking, remember? It leaves bruises."

"I'll kiss them better."

"I've got bruises everywhere."

"Then I shall kiss you everywhere." He didn't sound daunted at the prospect.

I knew I was lost. He had begun to rub his groin against mine. I closed my eyes. Then he undid my zip. His hand slipped inside my trousers, and he started to stroke my cock.

"Open your eyes."

I kept my eyes shut.

"Please, Adam, look at me."

Slowly, I opened my eyes. His face was tender and caring.

We kissed hungrily, and my desire made me ignore my bruised lips.

All too soon, I came.

We clung to each other like the survivors of a shipwreck.

Then I led him into the bedroom.

"Fuck!"

"Is that an order? You've not done this before, have you?"

"You're not the first."

"Liar!"

I began to cry.

He rocked me in his arms and told me it was all right.

"I wanted it to be special," I said.

"It *is* special," he comforted.

"It's not. It bloody hurt."

"That's my fault, not yours. We'll try again later," he promised.

But we didn't try later. He went out to buy a bottle of wine, and I left before he got back.

I gave people to understand I'd fallen down some steps. I didn't know if anyone believed me, but they soon stopped asking questions and put it out of their minds. Which was more than I could manage. I told myself that Pip was just some thug who meant nothing to me, but my own argument didn't convince me.

Eventually, I could stand it no more: I had to see him again. So I went round to the flat.

There was no reply when I knocked. A neighbor said they'd gone away.

My sense of loss was overwhelming.

A year later, I was in the area on business. Despite telling myself it was a waste of time, I walked up the three flights to Pip's flat and knocked.

There were footsteps; the door opened, and the young man standing there smiled at me.

It wasn't Pip.

"I'm sorry. I must have the wrong address." Overcome with despair, I turned and began to walk away.

Then I heard it: the sound of a flute. I turned back.

"Who's playing?" I asked eagerly, trying not to build my hopes up.

"*Un moment.*" The stranger disappeared back into the flat, and I heard snatches of an animated discussion.

A woman came to the door.

"Can I help you?"

I repeated my question.

"It's a CD belonging to my grandson."

"Pip?"

The woman stared curiously at me. "That's my name. My grandson is Philippe. It can be confusing."

"Is he here?"

"He's gone to Germany with the orchestra. They're due back at the end of the month. Are you Adam?"

I said I was.

Her expression softened. "He's often spoken of you. Would you like to come in?"

I was nervous; it had been a long time. But now the orchestra had returned to Britain, and I had to see Philippe, so I returned to the flat. As soon as Philippe opened the door, his eyes lit up. "Adam. I was afraid—"

And then we were in each other's arms.

"I had to come back," I said, as we lay in bed together. "When Edouard opened the door, I thought the worst—that you'd found someone else or that you'd disappeared forever. Even when your grandmother came to the door, I didn't recognize she was the woman in the paintings."

"I didn't think you wanted to see me again. Who could blame you? My companions had beaten you up, and I'd stood by and watched. I was frightened they might do the same to me."

"But they were your friends."

"No. I met them for the first time that evening. We'd had a few drinks together and were on our way to get a takeaway when they saw you. They were spoiling for a fight—anyone would have done. When your membership card to The Gay Blade fell out of your pocket, they had their motive. One that ensured I held my tongue."

"Why didn't you tell me this before?"

"I was ashamed and felt just as guilty as the others, maybe more so as I'd done nothing to prevent it. I felt as if I'd forfeited any right to your forgiveness."

"There's one thing I don't understand: what excuse did you give those two louts for not joining in?"

"I said I didn't want to injure my hands. I'd already told them I was a musician, although I let them think I was in a band."

"What now?"

Philippe grinned.

"I didn't mean *that*."

"I was planning on going to my grandmother's villa on the Côte d'Azur. She and Edouard are staying on here, so we'd have it to ourselves."

"You want *me* to come, too?"

"I'm taking the bike. You can ride pillion."

The thought of straddling a powerful motorbike, my arms wrapped around Philippe's waist, was both terrifying and deeply erotic. My cock hardened.

This time our lovemaking was an intoxicating mix of gentle and rough, slow and frantic; kisses, caresses, playful bites. Spent, I lay exhausted for a few minutes. Then I turned over onto my stomach.

Philippe kissed my neck. "It's all right," he whispered. "We don't have to."

I knew he was referring to our failed attempt at sex a year ago.

"It isn't all right yet," I said. "But it will be."

THE RED *MALO* (A POSTMODERN ISLAND ROMANCE)

David May

'Aikane, *now used to mean an honest and laudable friendship between two males, originally meant the vice of that burnt-up city.*

—Dr. Nathaniel Emerson, 1898

When President Palin's economic policies brought about the collapse of America's infrastructure, leading to the US military's evacuation from our islands, Hawai'i *nei* proclaimed its sovereignty, parliament reconvened, and our monarchy was restored after more than a century of occupation. With complex family systems that crossed cultures and color, and intermarriage being the norm, every *kupa* was seen as a vital part of the intricate and beautiful design that was to be Hawai'i *nei.* Only the missionary families left in droves, their fortunes built on stolen land that now reverted to the crown; the pineapple and sugarcane plantations occupying that royal land were nationalized.

In those heady early days of nationhood there was much work

to do, and all able hands came to do it. Even those of high birth came to rebuild the ancient fishponds, to gather the wild chickens and pigs for domestication and even to plow the fields to grow our traditional crops of taro, sweet potato, breadfruit and bananas. Food there was in abundance, but it had to be managed, and Jonas Kekoa Pali'uli Mea'ike was one of those educated men who understood how we could best feed our people.

The day I first met Jonas—after admiring him from a distance for some weeks—he wore a red *malo* of the finest *kapa*, indicating his status as a high chief. Many of us, which is to say the younger men, had, since the return of sovereignty, taken to wearing the *malo*, it being both practical and comfortable—but ours were made from whatever fabric we found. When rebuilding the ancient fishponds, as we were that day, our *malo* were often made from nothing more than the remnants of old T-shirts. *Kapa* was still precious and worn only on special occasions, or by those of high rank—like Jonas Mea'ike.

Jonas was *hapa*, like most Hawaiians, with an ancestry that included ancient chiefs and chieftesses, missionary stock and a successful Portuguese sea captain who had retired to Hawai'i and taken a young *ali'i* wife who claimed Kamapua'a as an ancestor. They were a large clan known for their wisdom and generosity as much as for their beauty and wealth.

On this day, Jonas was not just looking at the work being done under his supervision but was, at the moment I first saw him, descending into the fishpond to assist with some of the heavier lifting.

"*Kue!*" I yelled. "Your *malo* be ruined, cuz!"

He smiled as he looked at me, his teeth brilliant behind his beard, his eyes flashing laughter.

"Thanks, li'l brah, but the *malo* is less important than the work."

With that, he lent his shoulder to the task at hand, adding his own considerable strength to ours. When it was time for lunch, and I was leaving with the others, a strong, gentle hand settled on my shoulder. I turned to see Jonas's handsome face.

"Eat with me, Kawina."

How he had learned my name, I didn't know, but neither did I question him.

"*Mahalo*. My honor, brah."

We sat together under a tree and shared the same meal as the other men: poi, pork, native bananas and pineapple, all eaten with our hands off of a banana leaf. We ate in silence. I wondered what he wanted, but my nature being that of a follower, I waited for him to speak.

"You *kama'aina*, li'l brah?"

"Yeah, brah. I'm born Kahuku. My parents stay here before I'm born."

He smiled.

"You talk pidgin like you born stay here, brah."

"But I can talk like this too. I learned to speak my parents' English at home and pidgin with my friends. But here where we work, pidgin stay."

Jonas laughed.

"You're educated?"

I shrugged my shoulders.

"By my parents mostly. I read a lot, but I no stay school long."

He laughed again. And then he said, "We need men like you, Kawina, men we can raise up and show the world, men of all colors.... *I* need a man like you."

The last phrase caught me unawares, and something sweet and wonderful jumped inside me, stirring my *ule* to attention.

Mealtime over, the men dispersed. There were two shifts, one from dawn to late morning, the second from midafternoon to dusk. The midday hours were for rest, play and making love. Family obligations coming first, not everyone was expected to work both shifts. I normally worked both since I was, after an afternoon with my *moe 'aikane* followed by a nap, well prepared for that second shift. Only when my parents needed me did I miss either.

Some of the men stripped off their *malo* to bathe in the ocean; others found a shady place to rest until the evening shift; still others, with whom I was often included, found a secluded spot for sport fucking. Jonas and I watched the men swimming and wrestling naked in the water, their hard, muscular bodies glistening with sweat and brine in the brilliant light of Hawai'i *nei*. I felt another stir in my *malo*, and would've rearranged myself but for the presence of the chief sitting beside me. I turned my attention back to him when I felt his hand on my shoulder; something deep in my gut jumped with as much excitement as my *ule*. I returned his gaze.

"Shall we go for a walk, Kawina?"

I nodded my assent and we headed down the shore, away from where the other men were playing or napping. His arm around my shoulder, I leaned slightly against his body as we walked, feeling the full strength and power of his hairy, muscular body, one decorated with traditional tattoos of ancient design as exclusive to his family as a tartan is to a Scottish clan.

He spoke and I listened, though I can hardly remember now what we discussed. My heart and *ule* were too distracted to give him my complete attention. When we reached the far end of the sandy shore, he gently pulled me to him until our noses touched, a sign of intimacy between family members, friends or lovers.

"Kawina, I..."

Then he kissed me and I felt both our *ule* jump. His great arms wrapped around me. My heart raced.

He looked at me, disconcerted.

"We should get back," he said softly.

I followed. His arm was no longer around my shoulder; my hand was in his. We were silent until we came to where his car waited to take him home.

"*Aloha, kane nui.*"

"*Ho'alohaloha*, Kawina."

I watched him drive away before running to the water to clear my head and cool my body.

"Don' you know, brah?" a friend asked as I reached the water. "*Kane nui* gotta wife an' *ohana.*"

"Fo' real, brah?"

"Fo' real, but dat don' mean he don' like you. He ask 'bout you, wanna know yo' name an' *de kine*. Yeah, de *buggah* like you, brah."

This news of Jonas's wife and family was like a kick in the stomach, yet I hoped to see him again soon. I also knew that my heart was already his.

The next morning I looked anxiously for Jonas but didn't see him. I wondered if I had said or done something wrong, if I had offended him in some way and so lost him forever. A week passed and I thought I'd console myself with a tumble in the shade with my *mahu* friends.

"No way, brah. You belong to *ali'i*, now. We don' touch, brah. You *kapu* now."

"Brah, you think I'm Jonas's boy? Where Jonas stay? I dunno. I'm my own man, brah."

"No, brah. You *kapu* fo' sure. All *de kine* know dat."

"Yeah, brah. Soon you too high to work wit' us in de fish-ponds. Once you got his *ule* in you, den you *ali'i* stay."

I walked away confused and hopeful, but wondered what

my place would be in the life of a chief with an *ali'i* wife and a house full of children. By the old laws, I would be little more than a servant, a catamite. Things had changed, of course, but the powers and responsibilities of the remaining *ali'i* were still being debated by parliament, and I had no idea of where a *haoli* nobody like me could fit into the life of such a man. So pent up and with so much nervous energy to spend, I ran into the ocean, swimming as far out as I dared before returning to shore, too tired to worry about Jonas or the *kapu* that had been placed on me.

Later that evening, just as I stepped out of the shower and was looking at myself in the mirror wondering if I should shave or grow my beard (men rarely shaved more than twice a week on Hawai'i *nei*, even among the *ali'i*), there was a knock at the door. I scratched the week's stubble and went to answer in nothing but a clean *malo*.

"*Aloha,*" I said to the stranger in the silk aloha shirt and khaki shorts standing on the doorstep.

"*Aloha loa nui.* Are you Kawina Dawson?"

"Dat's me, brah. Who you?"

"I'm sent by Jonas Mea'ike. You are invited to dinner."

I put on my nicest threads, such as they were: a not too ratty aloha shirt, beach shorts and the cleanest pair of *slippahs* I could find. I was a working boy from a working family; there was no sense in pretending I was anything else, so I went to dinner unshaven but clean. That was about all he should expect on such short notice.

It had been years since I'd been in a car, even a small one. Normally I biked everywhere, or took the light rail train that circled and crossed over the island along the old highways. Private vehicles, even the most practical, were a luxury now; only a few of the *ali'i* and the monarch were seen in them and then only occasionally. It was not unusual to see even the royal family on public transportation with the rest of us, greeting us with informal smiles and an extended hand. Sitting in the seat next to the driver, I didn't attempt much in the way of small talk. I just watched the passing view as the small car made its way to Kailua.

The house was large for the islands and a short walk from the ocean. Facing the sea, it had been built to use our blessed trade winds to keep it cool year round. Once part of a large estate, I could see that the property's former lawns were now dedicated to raising food crops for the household. Semiwild chickens and pigs wandered about the grounds, seemingly content with their lot. A low hedge of *ti* plants bordered the walk. Wild orchids and flowering vines grew wherever there was space, allowed to flourish for the sake of their beauty and the sweetness they lend the air.

Just as I noticed the traditional *kahili* at either side of the great double door, it opened and out came Jonas in his red *malo* and an unbuttoned aloha shirt. His beard was freshly trimmed, accentuating a square jaw and high cheekbones. He opened his arms and held me close before brushing my lips with his own and touching his nose to mine.

"*Aloha,* Kawina, and welcome."

"*Aloha loa nui,*" I answered, not sure of how I ought to address him—by his first name or by some honorific? The rules had yet to be written for our new nation, and we were still finding our way between ancient traditions and the expectations of civilization.

His arm around my shoulder, he led me inside the elegant but simple home where we were greeted by a beautiful, statuesque woman in a tailored red silk *muumuu*, her hair brushed back and falling to her waist. She greeted me with a smile and two open hands that took mine.

"*Aloha*. You must be Kawina."

"Yes, Nenehiwa, this is Kawina. Jonas, my wife."

Though my hands were still in hers, I made a small bow.

"*Aloha loa nui, wahine nui*. I'm honored."

"Handsome and well mannered, Jonas. I see why you're so fond of him. Come outside and join the *luau* and meet our other guests."

His arm still around me, Jonas and I followed Nenehiwa into the garden where a *lanai* had been erected in honor of the occasion. The other guests were sitting comfortably on pillows and mats around a dais where a man and woman sat, clearly the guests of honor. As soon as I recognized them, I knelt on one knee, my head bowed. There was a sudden pause in the conversation as my obeisance was made.

"Please, rise, *kane*," the king said to me. "Come here and give us your *aloha*."

I did as asked, Jonas's firm hand on the small of my back holding me steady. The king rose, took my hands in his and touched his nose to mine.

"This is Kawina, *mo'i*."

"So I see. And I think we must approve of him."

Conversation resumed and I was seated next to Jonas where a beer and a plate overflowing with food were brought to me. I ate nervously, looking around at so much finery and beauty. These were the *ali'i* and I was eating with them, listening to their chatter, wishing I didn't look so shabby.

"You look fine," said Jonas as if reading my mind. "No one expects anyone to dress up. *Mo'i* himself is dressed in nothing but a *malo* and a shirt. Nenehiwa is only in her finest because of the occasion."

I nodded before looking him straight in the eye and asking:

"Is it true I'm *kapu, kane nui*? That's what they tell me at the fishpond."

Jonas leaned close and whispered in my ear: "Only if you want to be, Kawina, only if you want."

And then he kissed me.

No one seemed to take notice of the kiss, least of all Nenehiwa. She was far too busy flirting with the several men seated around her. These were the *ali'i*, I reminded myself, and traditionally allowed as many spouses and lovers as desired.

"Nenehiwa has given me six children, li'l brah—and at least two of them are mine," Jonas said softly, reading my mind once again. "She is free to love whom she may, as am I, Kawina. You are here so she might meet and approve of you. I want to give you more than my *ule*. I also want to give you my heart. I've watched you at the fishpond and see what a hard worker you are, how bright you are, how loyal you are to your friends."

I blushed at the flattery, looked down at the *lei* that he had put around my neck. His hand caressed my face, and I looked back into his eyes.

"And just as precious to me is your sense of what is right. You respect the *ali'i* but aren't overawed by them. You knelt as you should before *mo'i*, but were not afraid to give him your *aloha* when he asked you. I know I can trust you. I know you will not lie to me if I ask you if you love me."

"Love?" I asked, bewildered at this sudden revelation. "I thought you might like me, brah, and hoped you'd sport with me, but I didn't think you wanted more than that. This is too much too fast. Yes, I love you, Jonas, but what place would I have in your life? I would give you my all, but I know I can never be more than your plaything."

"That's not true, Kawina. You can and will be much more if you let me make you mine."

He kissed me again and my *ule* jumped. I would have reached for his if we hadn't been surrounded by so many other guests. I wanted to wrap my arms around him, to feel him inside me, to see his face in delicious anguish as he planted his seed in me. My mind raced; my heart jumped; and suddenly I felt something inside me protest this rush to something more serous than a tumble on the grass. I pulled away from him and looked him in the eye.

"Lift the *kapu*, Jonas. Lift the *kapu* and give me time to think. I don't know if I want you or just your *ule*. I know I want you, but let me decide."

"But how long, Kawina? A week, a month, a year?

"Let's measure time as the ancients did. Give me a lunar month to decide, but lift the *kapu* so I can make the choice for myself."

He accepted the wisdom of this with a nod.

"If you only knew how much I love you, Kawina."

When I went back to the fishpond I discovered that I'd been made foreman, a promotion I hoped I deserved. I worked just as hard, felt my muscles ache just as much at the end of the shift. I continued eating my meals with Jonas when he was there, but our affection never passed beyond more than an *aloha* and the touching of our noses. When Jonas was supervising elsewhere, I ate with my friends as before. They teased me about Jonas when they invited me to join them on the grass and I declined, feeling no impulse toward any man but Jonas Kekoa Pali'uli Mea'ike.

Some evenings he brought a picnic dinner that we ate on the beach, talking and laughing. He always commented on the moon's beauty but said no more about the passing of the lunar month or the *kapu* I had placed between us. I am not shy or afraid of a challenge, but I am docile by nature. My pleasure comes in service, and I knew I could be comfortable being in

Jonas's shadow. Perhaps he sensed that about me from the beginning. Perhaps he saw how eagerly I serviced my *moe 'aikane*. I never asked; I only knew that I loved him more as the weeks passed, that my trust in him was implicit.

On the last day of the lunar month, Jonas was not at the fishpond, now completed and being successfully farmed with me at the lead. This was not unusual since he supervised several sites and would need to spend more time at those being constructed than at completed ponds. When noon came, and I went into the shelter to eat and rest with the men I supervised, I looked around hoping for his arrival. When the next shift took over, I went back to the house on the former military base that I shared with some other *mahu*, knowing that they would tease me and ask me about Jonas. I hadn't told them about the *kapu*, but they saw how we looked at each other, saw how I smiled whenever I saw him. They saw but didn't understand how desperately I wanted Jonas or how important this test of my own fidelity was to me.

I lay down for a nap, thinking that I would help weed the neighborhood taro and potato patches later in the afternoon. I must have been more tired than I realized, because I fell sound asleep for some hours, waking with a start to see Jonas standing at my bedroom door in nothing but his red *malo*. The moon had risen and he was bathed in her blue light.

"*Aloha*, Jonas," I said stretching before rising from my bed, still naked, my *ule* at attention.

"*Aloha loa nui*, Kawina. Did you think I forgot what day it is?"

"I was afraid you were called away."

"And I was afraid of what you'd tell me today, so I had to see you alone."

"Is that why the house is empty, another *kapu*?"

He smiled.

"Can you blame me?"

He looked me in the eyes, honestly afraid I'd turn him away.

"Jonas, tell me where I am to sleep tonight."

He swept me in his arms and kissed me. We were evenly matched for height and breadth, neither of us small men, but he was still stronger than me. I undid his *malo* to see his *ule* reaching high like a rooster stretching its neck to crow. I knelt before what I so longed to possess. When I swallowed his seed, I would have his *mana*, and it would be a part of me forever.

I quickly became a part of his household, Uncle Kawina to the children, *muli poki'i* to Nenehiwa, and Mr. Kawina to the staff. I went to the fishpond most days. Sometimes I went with Jonas to the different worksites, acting as his assistant. Sometimes I worked in the family garden or minded the children, who accepted me with casual enthusiasm. Every night we made love, and every night his *mana* became a greater part of me, a secret I kept to myself lest I tempt his *'amakua* to strike me down.

One morning, after again making love, he asked me to bathe, something we normally did at the end of the workday. I was puzzled but obeyed, keeping my shower short as we were all asked to do. After breakfast I was led to a new *lanai* that had been made the day before. There, next to a pile of mats and *kapa* sheets, was a renowned tattoo artist, one well versed in the ancient designs unique to each *ali'i* family.

I knew what was expected of me and lay down on the mats while Jonas and the artist went over the exact placement of the designs that would forever mark me as his consort. The artist shaved and cleaned my skin and began. I winced but said nothing. The pain increased but then subsided as I was given small bits of *awa* to chew. This dulled all sensation and I felt at ease through most of the day, neither hungry nor thirsty, as the artist continued his work over my right pectoral, shoulder and upper arm. Periodically Jonas came to see how we were progressing, to give me sips of water and stroke my hair as his eyes looked into mine, overflowing with love and pride.

When it was over, I was ritually washed with seawater before heading to the bathroom, where Jonas gently cleansed and wrapped the wounded flesh in *ti* leaves and *kapa*, whispering words of encouragement. I ate a small meal and went to bed though it was still light and slept through the next morning.

I awoke hungry and thirsty and wondering where Jonas was. I rose stiffly and was trying to dress myself when Nenehiwa came in wearing nothing but a *pa'u*, her breasts exposed.

"*Muli poki'i,* you are awake at last, but in time for lunch."

I made no attempt to hide my nakedness from her, she having already seen all of me when I bathed in the outdoor shower, or swam with her children. Gently she helped me into a loose-fitting shirt and gym shorts I had occasionally seen Jonas wear at the beach.

"Welcome to the family, *muli poki'i.* Now you are one of us. Now you share our *mana.*"

I thanked her and accepted her assistance as we walked slowly to a large lunch that I devoured as if I hadn't eaten in days.

A *kahuna* came daily to redress the tattooed skin, muttering incantations as he worked. When Jonas returned home he held me gently in his arms, hesitating to make love for fear I was too tender to respond. But I wanted him as much as before, wanted more of the *mana* that we shared. In a few days I was back at work in the garden or swimming with the children, my upper body always covered in a loose shirt. Jonas told me that there would be more tattoo work on my lower body, but that would come later.

* * *

Months passed, the moon showed her light on our love, and I could not imagine myself happier than I was being a part of my new *ohana*. My own family came to visit, staying for several days so my mother could fuss over me, my father say how proud he was of me, and my brothers and I could roughhouse as we always had before, this time joined by Jonas and the children.

One evening, after our usual afternoon nap and lovemaking, Jonas and I bathed together as we often did. We dried each other and Jonas handed me a new *malo*, a beautiful *kapa malo* worked with intricate designs. Dumbfounded, I looked at him to be sure that it was me he intended to wear it. He smiled and nodded, a small laugh escaping from the handsome bearded mouth I loved to kiss. Then he took a small *kapa* cape, worked in the same designs as the *malo,* and tied it around my shoulders.

I helped him dress in his red *malo* and a red *kapa* cape much longer than mine. Wordlessly, I followed him to the waiting car that took us to the Iolani Palace, a place I had only seen before as a school-aged visitor. Now there was a reception being given by the *mo'i* and his wife, who greeted us at the door. We exchanged *aloha,* and *lei* were slipped over our necks by their own royal hands as we bowed. I marveled that I, a poor *haoli* with little education, was there at all.

I accepted the wine that Jonas handed to me and looked around, awed at the simple splendor of the palace. I noted that not only were the *ali'i* and other prominent citizens at the reception, but the official envoys sent from Australia, the United Kingdom, the Netherlands, Japan, Canada and the new nation of Cascadia. Nenehiwa was there in another beautiful *muumuu*, her hair dressed with flowers, being escorted by a handsome *hapa*. She greeted us from across the room with a smile and a nod.

I followed Jonas around the room, my hand in his, trying not to be overwhelmed but not wanting to be blasé, either. I smiled, proud to be here with Jonas, proud to be accepted as his consort.

Four *kahuna* entered the room chanting *mele*, escorted by four *koa* carrying *kahili*. They were lead by the *kuhina nui*, a dignified, older woman dressed in white *kapa*, her back as straight as a cliff, her face as luminescent as the moon. We all stood attentively, listening to the ancient chants that only a few in the room truly understood. When they had done, the *kuhina nui* addressed the party.

"Our blessed *mo'i*, with the agreement of the *ali'i* represented by the House of Nobles, has graciously chosen to honor the following women and men with the status and title of *ali'i* in thanks for the work they have done, and will continue to do, for our nation, so that they may always be honored by our people...."

As each name was called, the honored person came forward and was decorated with a *lei* of precious red and yellow feathers, the kind from which the *ali'i* once made their capes and helmets. Among the eight names she called, mine was the last. I was too startled to respond. Jonas pushed me forward and I bowed before the *kuhina nui*.

"Young Kawina, I acknowledge you as the favored consort of Jonas Kekoa Pali'uli Mea'ike. You are not his husband for that would infer that equality existed between you, now being honored, and one of ancient lineage. You are a consort, but may have all the expectations of a spouse in regards to your happiness and welfare. Jonas may not take another spouse or consort except with the consent of the High Chieftess Nenehiwa and you, Kawina.

"Some will say that a man like Jonas Kekoa Pali'uli Mea'ike

should not have such a consort, but they forget our history. The ancient king Liloa loved his *'aikane*, and a man no less than Kamehameha the Great had his *moe 'aikane* with whom he shared his *mana*. This is right."

I accepted the precious feather *lei* with a trembling heart.

"You will now be known as Mea'aloha Mea'ike, the Beloved of Jonas Kekoa Pali'uli Mea'ike."

With tears in my eyes, amid the applause, I returned to Jonas and his embrace. He held me close, kissing away my tears.

"This is right, Mea'aloha. You will always be my favorite *'aikane*, my one great love."

And so I was.

Hawaiian and Pidgin Glossary

I'm told that as a child I spoke pidgin, the unofficial language of Hawai'i. I don't recall speaking it so much as being constantly corrected when we moved to the mainland. I have tried to capture the rhythm of pidgin but will not pretend that the pidgin recorded here is wholly accurate. Words and phrases below are Hawaiian, pidgin or both. I am not a scholar in either language and beg the indulgence and goodwill of those more knowledgeable, and ask them to remember that whatever the errors, they are made with aloha nui.

'Aikane: Usually translated as "bosom friend." *Moe 'aikane* might be translated as fuckbuddy.

Ali'i: Chief or chieftess; the *ali'i* are the ancient nobility, once thought to have divine ancestry.

Aloha: Love, affection, with love. Used for "hello," "goodbye" and "amen."

'Amakua: Family god, often an animal deity, from whom an

ali'i family claimed descent.

Awa: A medicinal plant with narcotic qualities.

Brah: Bro', short for *braddah*; a polite form of address between male peers.

Buggah: A fellow, any male, usually used in the third person.

Cuz: Cousin; a polite form of address toward another islander.

De kine: The kind: this or that, whatever, the right stuff, what it is, et cetera.

Haoli: Any foreigner but usually referring to those of northern European ancestry. It is not a derogatory word in itself; it depends on how it's used.

Hapa: Half; people of mixed ancestry.

Hawai'i nei: *This* Hawai'i as opposed to other islands or island groups with the same or similar name.

Ho'alohaloha: An expression of affection.

Kahili: Tall feathered fans used to designate the home or presence of an *ali'i*.

Kahuna: Wise one; applied to men or women.

Kama'aina: Local, native born.

Kamapua'a: Literally "Pig Man." Kamapua'a is a demigod who inhabits O'ahu. He takes the form of a handsome, hairy muscular man—or a great, black boar.

Kane: Man

Kapa: Tapa cloth made from beaten bark, used for clothes and bedding.

Kapu: Taboo, forbidden. Sacred.

Kawina: A Hawaiian transliteration of "Kevin," one of many neo-Hawaiian names (like *Kawika* for David) popular today.

Kekoa: Brave one.

Koa: Warrior

Kue: Untranslatable. Roughly: "Hey, look out!" or "Hey, you!" when yelled; or "Who's there?" or "Are you there?" when said softly.

Kuhina nui: Prime minister; historically an appointed position, usually a woman, expected to balance the *moi's* will with reason.

Kupa: Citizen, native.

Lanai: An open, shaded structure; traditionally a temporary one erected for special occasions or guests of honor.

Lei: A necklace or wreath, made from flowers, seeds, shells or feathers.

Luau: A feast, often in honor of a person or event.

Mahalo: Thank you.

Mahu: Queer: gay, lesbian, transgendered, intersexed. Like *haoli*, not a derogatory word but sometimes used derisively.

Malo: Traditional loincloth worn by Hawaiian men.

Mana: Power, life force, divine essence.

Mea'aloha: Beloved

Mea'ike: A person of authority.

Mele: Traditional chants, often celebrating genealogies and historical events.

Mo'i: Monarch

Muli poki'i: Youngest sibling.

Muumuu: Originally a shapeless dress introduced by the missionaries in response to the Hawaiians' casual nudity; it has evolved into a variety of long dresses worn by many Hawaiian women today, some of them elegant and richly made.

Nenehiwa: Precious

Nui: Great, very much, a lot.

Ohana: Family, extended family.

Pali'uli: A mythical paradise.

Pa'u: Traditional skirt of leaves or *kapa*.

Slippahs: Flip-flops

Stay: Any form or variation of the verb "to be."

Ti: A medicinal plant brought to Hawai'i by the ancient Polynesians.

Ule: Penis

Wahine: Woman

FOOL'S MATE

Shanna Germain

For almost a week, I didn't know; partly because I didn't *really* look at him, partly because even if I had looked, I wouldn't have seen. I came out of my dad's cabin on the morning of each of those days, and the man was already sitting at the picnic table in the shared yard space between the cabins, chessboard open and half-played in front of him. He was Kilway, my father's work friend, or friendly neighbor, or hated enemy, depending on the state of my father when he mentioned him.

Big shouldered, sporting a crew cut tinged with gray, Kilway raised his hand off the ebony queen and waved as I came down the porch stairs. When I waved back, he nodded and lowered his hand to the queen's crown. Each movement deliberate, on purpose.

That summer, my father called me Puppy or, when he was in a good mood, Pup, because I couldn't hold still, couldn't seem to get from one place to the next without losing my feet. He told me my equilibrium was out of balance, 'cause I'd moved from one side of the country to the other, 'cause I'd switched from living with a mom to living with a dad. Also, because I was supposed to have gone to college, but that got switched up on me too, on account of the divorce and nobody having any money.

On the phone, my mom said that it was just teenage pains and that I would grow out of it, but by that point, she only told the truth when she wasn't drinking, and she said "painsh," so I didn't dare believe her. It was Kilway, with his careful muscles and his bones slow through the air, that gave me some kind of hope for the future.

"You play, son?" he'd asked on the first day. A father who never called me anything but nicknames, most of them animals—Pup, Dodo, Pussy—and this man I'd never seen before calling me son. If my equilibrium was messed up already, it was more so now. Kilway was older than me, but not as old as my dad, and around him I wanted to be my best self, my most grown-up being.

"I do, a bit," my consonants carefully pronounced.

"Come then," he said, as though I had answered no. "I'll teach you."

As I moved toward the picnic table, the grass reached up and tangled my laces, knocked my ankles together until I had to grab the top of the table to stay upright. The chess pieces danced into new squares, and I heard Kilway's laugh for the first time. If his body made me want to be an adult, his laugh made me want to crawl inside him and haunt the space that made that sound, to take it for my own.

"Hmm," he said. "We might have more in common than I thought."

Watching him watch me, my blood made my ears so hot I wasn't sure I heard him right. I put one leg carefully through the space between the bench and the table and then the other. I lowered myself into the seat across from him, making sure my knees did not touch his. I noticed them, though; his thin legs leaned sideways against the bench, clad in jeans despite the heat.

Kilway turned the board so the ebony pieces were in front of me. They were made of wood, and the grain shone through in the necks and heads of the horses. Kilway set up his pieces, white wood the same color as his fingers, grains and fingerprints in the same swirled patterns. Under his careful fingers, each piece landed directly in the center of its square.

"Chess is about planning, logic, thinking ten steps ahead," he said. "Must know what your opponent's thinking."

I listened, tried to center my pieces on their squares, but I knocked over my king. Kilway either didn't notice or was kind enough to not comment if he did.

We played three games of chess that day. I lost every time. Not because he was better than me—he *was* better than me, his every move was careful and planned—but because every time his hand made its move across the table toward me, my ears went hot all over again and my feet tangled under the table even though they weren't trying to get anywhere else. The third game, he beat me in less than five moves. Bam-bam-bam-bam-bam.

"You'll get it," he said. And for some reason—maybe the way he talked, maybe that quiet, controlled stillness—for some reason, I believed him.

Later that night, I lay in my bed listening to my dad and Kilway clink beers and laugh out in the yard. I closed my eyes, and images of Kilway's fingers on the head of his king wouldn't leave my head. His fingers tightened and slid down the chess piece, from crown to body. Back up. And then, in my mind, Kilway, too, rose and walked to my side of the table. He bent over me until his breath brushed the back of my neck. He put his hands slowly into the air until they met the skin of my arms and rested there. My body ached and shuddered at the image, while outside Kilway laughed at something my father said.

It went on like that for nearly three weeks, Kilway and me sitting across the table from each other, with my body turning hot every time he looked at me, swept one of my pieces off the table or reached across the board with his careful hands.

I'd been with my dad for twenty days by then. That night, he came onto the porch, his arms crisscrossed over the blue T-shirt he wore on his days off, as I slid my queen right up against a checkmate.

"You're gonna' lose again, Pup," he said, as though he'd been standing there watching me lose for all those days already and not working down at the salt mine. Every night, he'd come home a grayish-white color and smelling like tears. I thought that had been a smell that belonged only to my mom and me, but now I saw that it was everywhere. I thought maybe it was a smell that would follow me my whole life, one of those accidents of genetics that you were stuck with forever.

"Kilway, why don't you come over for dinner?" my dad called. "I'm grilling steak on the Barbie-doll, and we'll test Pup's salad-making skills."

My hand pinched the crown of my queen, while I waited to see what Kilway would say. Part of me wanted him to say no—he was something, one thing that felt like mine here in this space of my father. And part of me wanted him to say yes, so I could hold on to him longer, see him do something besides sit at the picnic table and whomp me in chess.

"We'll have to eat out here," Kilway said, tapping his fingers in a deliberate rhythm against the side of his thigh. His smile was something I hadn't seen before, a half curve at the side of his mouth, his lips staying closed like they held a secret. "If that would be all right with you."

I moved my queen forward to butt against Kilway's king, but my hand shook. When I placed the piece down, every still-standing piece on the table trembled.

"Yeah, yeah," my dad waved a hand in the air. His movement had none of Kilway's care, so his hand flopped between his shoulder and his belt buckle, pushing the air aside as it went. "I know, I know, you always need something." But my dad said it in the way that he sometimes talked to the dogs when they pushed against his legs and he rubbed their ears as they whined to go out. Not the way I'd heard him talk to my mother when she needed something—money, school clothes, a place for me to stay for the summer.

Kilway's answering voice was something I hadn't heard before either, and I maybe believed my dad for once, that maybe he and Kilway were friends of sorts. And maybe enemies a little bit too. And all of that seemed to be okay between them.

"Yeah," Kilway said as he picked up his king. "And you always got something to give."

Dinner was burnt steak, some wilted spinach that I mixed with Italian dressing, and bottles of beer. The beer was the best part. I had another year before I was legal to drink, and the cold liquid tasted good in my mouth for that reason alone, because otherwise it just tasted like shit.

We ate without talking, the way I was learning that men do, my dad next to me, Kilway sitting on his side of the bench. In the heat and silence, the dogs panted on the porch, waiting until my father would stand and stretch and put down his plate for their leftovers.

Dad rose before I was finished. There wasn't much meat left

for the dogs—between the three of us, we'd cleaned it out good. In the near dark, Dad scraped the burnt bits off the grill with his jackknife and wiped it on a paper plate.

"Kilway, you gonna' get off your ass and help with the cleanup, since I cooked?" The way my dad talked to him that night was—I didn't have a word for it, but it made me feel like I was intruding, pitcher-ears my mom used to say, even though he wasn't talking about anything but domestic stuff. It wasn't like lovers, not that I'd had many—a few girls who liked me well enough for a night and one boy who'd taken me in his mouth and then cried—but it was a sound I'd heard sometimes by accident, that way couples jostled, like poking each other with steak knives that were no longer sharp.

"He is a funny, funny man, your father," Kilway said low to me across the picnic table. To my dad, he shouted, "No, but I thought I'd come over later and take out your garbage."

I took a swig of my beer and let the bitter brew slide down my throat. I couldn't figure the turn things were taking, Kilway and my dad so friendly-like, bantering about shit that I either couldn't follow or that I didn't know. It made my feet feel ready to trip me up, even sitting still.

"Pup, get your new friend to pull his weight around here," my dad said, wiping his hands clean on a towel. "I'm tired of carrying his sorry ass." But I could tell he didn't mean it from the way he pulled another beer out of the cooler and handed it to Kilway.

Kilway held the bottle the same way he held his pawns: two fingers tight around the neck. And when he put it to his lips, I felt a shiver in my belly that I thought maybe meant I'd had too much beer. But at the same time, I knew it was something else. It was seeing those lips against the open mouth of that bottle, the way they circled. It was seeing something that I'd known a long time but hadn't known at all.

Dark came on as we sat there. My dad took one long last swallow of his beer.

"'Bout ready?" my dad asked. At first, I thought he was talking to me.

It was Kilway who answered.

"Ayet," he said in what sounded like he was clearing his throat, but that I could tell was some kind of yes. "If you don't mind." Kilway reached around to the side of the table and did something in the dark that I couldn't quite see. There was a small metallic clank and then another.

My dad did something next I never thought I'd see him do in his life. He bent down and let Kilway wrap his arms around him, Kilway's big arms going right around my dad's neck. I sat with my mouth half-open, dribbling out beer. My first thought was, *He's like me.* My second thought was, *What the hell does that mean?*

I didn't have a third thought because my dad lifted Kilway up and carried him. Carried him like he maybe used to carry me before he came out here to the other coast, before I was what I thought meant too big to be carried. My dad grunted a little under Kilway's weight but didn't falter. He just picked him up and put him down again. I saw what I hadn't before: the metallic clunks had been a wheelchair, unfolding.

"Oh, shit, David," Kilway said to my dad. "Look at that boy's face. He didn't know."

I didn't know how he could tell, in the almost dark. Something in my eyes maybe. Or the way my chin held itself, my nose full of the scent of burnt meat and falling night.

"You're the one's been playing chess with him three weeks straight," my dad said. "Figured it was your job to say something if you were gonna'."

"I'll say good night to you boys, is what I'll say," Kilway said. And then, slow and careful, he put his hands on the wheels of his chair and pushed himself toward his place.

I could tell my dad wanted to talk to me about it, although what he'd say, I didn't know. I felt stupid for not knowing, for not seeing what was right in front of me, and my face was hot in a way that was different than the way Kilway's touch made my skin heat.

I thought I wouldn't fall asleep dreaming of Kilway that night, but I did. And this time it was me rising from the bench, making my way around the table without fumbling my feet. Me leaning over Kilway, daring to put my hands against the back of his neck. My mouth too, my lips against that place where his hair curled just so against his skin.

I didn't say anything to my dad. And I sure didn't say anything to Kilway. Just showed up the next morning with my feet tangling me up in the grass. The chessboard was in front of him, but it was empty, all the pieces still crashed on their sides in the box. For the first time, I could notice the way Kilway's leaned legs didn't move from the bench and how the folded silver chair glinted in the morning sun as it lay against the side of the table.

He saw me looking at it.

"Your dad helps me out in the mornings and at night sometimes," he said. "I have a lady who comes, helps me with the rest."

I didn't ask the rest of what. I didn't know how.

He set the pieces up, his and mine, and then we played in silence. For the first time ever, not a word passed between us, playing steady until there was nothing left for me to do but settle his king.

"Check," I said.

When I went to move my piece, he caught my hand. It was the first time we'd touched. His warm wood-grained fingers sent my heart down between my legs.

"You can ask me about it," he said.

My mouth was somewhere else in my body too, because I couldn't seem to find my tongue.

"Motorcycle accident," he said, as though I'd actually asked. "Cliché, I know, but that's what life becomes, I think, if you live it long enough. Even if you fight against it. Hell, 'specially if you fight against it."

His hand was still on mine. Three fingers pressed into the back of my hand, holding down my heart, my tongue. Only my heartbeat rose, thick and quick with blood, and spurred me into making a move of my own.

I pushed myself up to lean across the table and touched the soft curve of his lips with my own, the scent of him in my breath. For a moment, it was the two of us, touching that way, his hand still on mine, closing soft around it. I thought I could feel the swirls of his fingertips, the soft ripples of his mouth. I wavered, strengthened in his touch, until nothing was dizzy, nothing would ever trip me up again. The pieces wiggled and fell on the board beneath me, toppling in a series of slow sounds.

Kilway's fingers shifted, slid up in that careful way of moving, found the base of my chin and held it as he looked at me. Those eyes, yes, but I wanted his hands. I wanted that touch to move me, slow and careful, the way he moved the chess pieces. To manipulate me and bend me, each angle and square.

"Son," Kilway said. "Oh, son, it's not like that. It's, well, it's me and your dad."

The bench knocked the air and vision out of me when I sat or fell, so that my breath came hard when it came at all. Kilway's white king was the only piece still standing, that stupid crown. I swept it off the board with the back of my hand, not even waiting to hear it clatter.

That night, when my dad came home, I could hear him and Kilway talking outside. There wasn't any laughter, no clinking of glass against glass. Just that quiet kind of talk that is so low it sounds like grass moving, like something that's only for the darkness to hear.

I lay in bed and made plans. I would get a job, a real one. I would go to college on my own. I would live in the middle, somewhere between the coasts, and never be split again.

I didn't hear my father come in, but I could smell him, straight from the mines.

"Pup," he said. "Puppy. I'm sorry. I didn't know."

I lay as still as I could, only opened one eye a slit so I could see him through the bars of my lashes. He was kneeling beside the bed, his skin covered in crystalline shards that made him almost glow. He smelled like salt and sweat and tears. Or maybe that was both of us: the shared genetics, the way misery followed us like an unseen hand, always planning to capture our hearts.

FIRST ROACH POND

Martin Delacroix

I don't believe in serendipity. I think all things happen for a reason.

Do you?

A lightning bolt snaked across the night sky, highlighting white-caps on First Roach Pond. A thunderclap followed; it shook my cottage. Above the dining table a propane lantern swayed from a ceiling hook, casting shadows onto knotty pine walls while, outside, saplings trembled in the gale.

My cottage sat on a ridge overlooking the lake, with a lawn sloping toward the shore. A row of double-hung windows faced the water, offering a pleasant vista during daytime: the lake, evergreens on the opposite shore and, beyond, several granite-peaked mountains. But at night I saw little besides moonlight reflecting off the lake's surface.

Viewed from an airplane, First Roach looked like a Rorschach blot: seven miles long, two miles wide, with jagged shorelines.

At the lake's northwest corner was Kokadjo, the village closest to me, with a general store, gas station, post office and motel. The nearest town was Greenville, twenty-three miles away, and our community's isolation rendered cell phones useless.

Now, as I stood at my windows and listened to rain drum my roof, I saw a beam of light cut through darkness, down at the shore, and I squinted in disbelief. Who'd be out on a night like this? My nearest neighbor, Raymond Devine, lived a quarter mile north, and Ray knew better than to venture out during a storm like this. The beam swung here and there, a yellow cone piercing the downpour.

Another lightning bolt flashed, revealing a powerboat I didn't recognize. Tied to the end of my dock, it pitched and rolled in the froth. A fellow in a ball cap and rain poncho made his way toward my cottage, ascending the slope with some difficulty. Twice he slipped and fell.

I greeted my visitor on my covered front porch. I'd left the cottage door open, and the propane lantern's glow cast a yellow rhombus onto the planks. He climbed my porch steps, then removed his cap and shook it. His dark hair was plastered to his head and a drop of rain glistened at the tip of his nose.

"Sorry to disturb you," he said, his voice a syrupy baritone, "but this storm came up awfully quick."

I said I had to agree. Thirty minutes before, all had been calm and dry.

He pointed to the lake. "I'm staying at O'Connor's. You know it?"

I nodded. O'Connor's was a fishing camp on the other side of the lake, a two-mile trip by boat from my place.

"You're shivering," I said, "come inside."

Unlacing his mud-caked hiking boots, he kicked them off and left them on the porch along with his poncho. He wore a flannel shirt and blue jeans, both drenched and clinging to his lanky frame. "My name's Gordon Noyle," he said, extending his hand.

I'm six-two and he was half a head shorter than me. Fair-skinned, with dark eyes, he looked close to my age. (I was twenty-three.) Stubble dusted his chin and jaw.

While we shook I told him I was James Beauregard. "But," I said, "friends call me Beau."

Gordon nodded. "If it's okay, I'll wait here till the weather calms down."

I fetched a flannel robe and a clean towel, then I showed Gordon the bathroom. "Get out of your clothes and we'll dry them."

Minutes later he sat on my sofa, sipping from a beer bottle, legs crossed at the ankles while his shirt and jeans, socks and briefs, lay atop my oil-burning heater, steaming.

He said, "I feel like an idiot, getting caught on the water like that."

"You were fishing?"

He puckered one side of his face and shook his head. "I went for a moonlight cruise, then the weather turned bad and..." he shrugged, "...here I am."

I didn't say anything.

His gaze traveled about the room. "This place is nice. Is it yours?"

I nodded. "My folks bought it years ago. We're from Florida."

Gordon joined his hands behind his head, elbows jutting. Outside, the storm raged. Another lightning bolt flashed, followed by a thunderclap, and Gordon shook his head as he stared out a window.

"You may be here awhile," I said.

He looked at me and blinked a time or two. "Sorry if I'm intruding."

I told him I was glad for the company. "Last time I spoke to anyone was...when? Yesterday, I guess, when I bought groceries. It gets lonely up here."

Gordon snickered. "I have the opposite problem."

"What's that?"

"I'm the oldest of six kids. Solitude's hard to come by when I'm home."

Gordon explained he was a University of Maine student, majoring in forestry. This fall he'd start his senior year. His family had rented two cabins at O'Connor's—they would stay three weeks—and they were driving him nuts.

"I'm used to living in Portland now, with my own apartment. Here there's no privacy and nothing to do but fish or hike in the woods."

He asked about me and I said I was a middle-school teacher, free for the summer. I'd been here two weeks, I told him, and I'd stay another month, until mid-August.

Gordon shifted his weight on the sofa and cracked his knuckles. "Don't you get bored, staying here alone?"

I shrugged. "My dad's paying me to reshingle the roof and paint the outside of the house; it's a lot of work and it keeps me busy. Evenings I read or listen to a ball game on the radio." Yawning, I said, "I'm usually in bed by ten, awake by six."

Gordon glanced at his wristwatch. "I'm keeping you up, aren't I?"

I told him it wasn't a problem. "Look," I said, "this storm won't quit anytime soon. Why not use my house phone? Call the O'Connor's office and let your folks know you're okay. You can spend the night on the sofa."

He arched his eyebrows. "You don't mind?"

"Nah."

While he placed the call I went to the bedroom, fetching Gordon a T-shirt and a pair of flannel sleep pants, a blanket and pillow.

"This is all very kind of you," he said when he hung up.

I figured he'd visit the bathroom to change, but instead he removed the robe and handed it to me and, right off, my mouth grew sticky at the sight of his slim physique, his dark pubic bush and his bulging genitals. I found it hard to swallow while he pulled the T-shirt over his head and his uncut cock wagged before him. His foreskin was buff-colored, his nuts plump in their furrowed sac.

"I'm handy with a paintbrush," he said, stepping into the sleep pants and pulling them up his legs. "I can swing a hammer, too. So if you want help, let me know; I'll work cheap."

I nodded, thinking, *An extra pair of hands would speed things up. Plus he's cute and I'd sure enjoy the company.*

I told him we'd discuss it in the morning.

While Gordon stretched out on the sofa, I turned off the propane lantern and the room grew dark. Switching on a flashlight, I wished Gordon a good night.

"Sleep well, Beau," he said. "Thanks again, for everything."

Gordon and I watched a guy with a forklift lower a pallet of shingles into the bed of my pickup truck. We'd driven to Greenville after spending our morning nailing tarpaper to the cottage's plywood sheathing, both of us scampering about the roof, wearing tool belts and swinging hammers, our lips stuffed with roofing nails.

Gordon seemed as comfortable on the roof as he would be on my sofa. "My dad's a building contractor," he told me; "I've been around construction all my life."

We'd already spent a week together, scraping loose paint, sanding and caulking the cottage's clapboard siding. It was the kind of work lending itself to talking, and conversation flowed easily between us. I was only a year older than Gordon, and we shared many interests: the Red Sox, '70s rock music, novels by Michael Chabon, Western omelets, cheese doodles and beer.

Lots of beer.

Since Gordon said he didn't own a car, each morning I'd drive to O'Connor's and pick him up. He'd meet me at the camp office, clutching a thermos of coffee and a sandwich wrapped in cellophane, then we'd work on the cottage till five in the afternoon, taking a lunch break at noon.

My dad kept a pair of baseball gloves at the cottage, and after a day's labor Gordon and I would play catch in the yard while the sun dipped behind the tree line, both of us swigging from beer bottles and talking on any number of subjects: world events, school, last night's Red Sox game, travel experiences, drinking feats, our plans for the future. Then I'd drive Gordon home.

"Lumber's big in Maine," he told me during one of our drives. "Most of the state is forest. I hope to land a job with a paper company 'cause they pay well and it's clean, easy work."

Now, at the building supply store in Greenville, I closed my truck's tailgate. After I signed a receipt for the shingles, we drove down Lily Bay Road, the highway leading to First Roach Pond. Afternoon sunlight entered the truck's cab through the rear window, reflecting off chrome trim on the dashboard. We both put on sunglasses. I flicked on the radio to a Bangor rock station, and Gordon slapped the passenger doorsill, keeping time with the music. He wore a ball cap, long sleeve T-shirt, saggy blue jeans and thick-soled work boots. He'd pushed his shirtsleeves up to his elbows, displaying his sinewy forearms and the fine, dark hair dusting them.

In the days we'd worked together, I found myself more and more attracted to Gordon, to his lanky frame, compact buttocks and big hands. His hair was thick and wavy, growing over the tops of his ears. He didn't shave often, and his stubble gave him a masculine look I found appealing; it contrasted nicely with his fair skin. His lips were full, as red as raw beefsteak. He had a habit of licking the corners of his mouth while he worked, and I sometimes wondered how it might feel to kiss him, to taste his tongue in my mouth.

Back in Florida, during college, I'd had a few boyfriends. Nothing serious, I'd never been in love, but I clearly liked men, and shortly after I graduated, when my mom asked why I hadn't dated girls at school, I explained. After that, neither she nor my dad inquired about my personal life.

Now, I taught English at a private school and my hours were long. I didn't just teach: I coached the girls' softball team, served as advisor to the school's newspaper staff, sat on several faculty committees. Weekdays I arrived at school at seven A.M. and I often did not leave until early evening. Saturdays I wrote lesson plans, ran errands, bought groceries and dined with my folks, then I drove home and crashed on the sofa, usually falling asleep with the television on. I had no time for a private life, and when I met Gordon I hadn't been laid in over two years. Sex for me was a magazine, a tube of jelly and my right hand. I was too busy for a boyfriend, I told myself.

But now, up in Maine, when I climbed under the covers at night, thoughts of Gordon filled my head. I'd lie in the dark and stare at the ceiling, recalling how I'd seen Gordon's belly button and the waistband of his underwear when he stood on a ladder, caulking overhead trim. Or I'd think about the night I'd first met him, when he took off the robe and I saw him naked. The memory made my cock stir each time it entered my thoughts.

Gordon had never mentioned dating; he didn't ogle girls when we saw them in Greenville or Kokadjo. He never asked me if I had dated or if I had a girlfriend, as most straight guys would do, and I found myself wondering if he might also be gay.

Now, as we left the highway with our load of shingles, I stole a glance at Gordon's crotch while we trundled down the gravel road leading to my cottage. The head of his cock bulged in his jeans and I licked my lips. How would it feel to lower his zipper and tease his dick till it hardened? How would his crotch smell when I lowered my face to his lap and sucked him off? And what would his come taste like?

Between my legs my own cock stiffened.

Careful, Beau.

By the time we'd unloaded the shingles the sun had set and the air had cooled. It was Friday, and when I asked Gordon what his plans were for the evening he looked at me like I was nuts.

"Same thing as always: I'll watch TV with my family."

Go ahead, ask...

"Why not stay here tonight? We can kill a case of beer and I'll make us dinner."

He glanced at the lake, then returned his gaze to me. "Sounds great," he said. "You're sure I'm not intruding?"

"Oh, hell no."

Gordon went inside and called O'Connor's, then we sat on the edge of my dock, our legs dangling while we sipped from beer bottles, watching light drain from the sky. Already a few stars appeared in the east and the only sound was crickets chirping. The air was still, the lake's surface smooth as a mirror. In the distance, mountain peaks glowed, the sun's last rays burnishing their granite faces.

"I sure envy your freedom," Gordon said, his gaze fixed on the water. "Must be nice, having this place to yourself."

I said, "I like it here, but sometimes I get lonely."

He shook his head. "Since we came to O'Connor's I've felt suffocated. My folks are always on my case."

"About what?"

He snorted. "You name it: 'Stand up straight. Why don't you shave? You need a haircut. No wonder you don't have a girlfriend.'"

I drank from my bottle, thinking, *Go on, ask him.*

I said, "Do you *want* a girlfriend?"

He shrugged and didn't say anything, his gaze still fixed on the water.

"Ever *had* a girlfriend?" I asked.

He looked at me and shook his head. "How about you?"

I told him no.

Dinner that night was two pickles and a bag of barbeque-flavored potato chips. By ten P.M. we had consumed three six-packs, and both of us were unsteady on our feet. The radio blared a 1980s song by an Australian rock group, AC/DC. We danced in our stocking feet in my living room, hopping about, jabbing the air with our fists, both of us clutching beer bottles. Gordon wore his ball cap backward. The propane lantern cast our silhouettes upon a wall—a pair of frantic, leaping shadows.

"You're a crappier dancer than me," Gordon shouted.

I grinned and shot him the bird, then I spun around a time or two before losing my balance and falling to the floor, spilling my beer and leaving me flat on my back, blinking at the ceiling.

Bending at the waist, Gordon shook his head and cackled. "You're shit faced," he cried.

I got on my knees, then rose to my feet, concentrating on keeping my balance.

The AC/DC tune ended, then a different song began, a Rod

Stewart number, slow and romantic. Gordon raised his chin and guzzled the last of his beer. His Adam's apple pumped and my pulse raced, just looking at him. Feeling horny and reckless, I extended an arm toward Gordon, my hand upturned.

"Come dance with me," I said.

He looked at my hand, then at me, and he giggled. "All right, Beau-Beau; if you want."

And I thought, *Beau-Beau? No one's ever called me that before.*

Setting his beer bottle aside, he approached. I put my arms around his waist and he did the same to me. Our hip bones met and Gordon rested his chin on my shoulder. We swayed to the music, shuffling our feet, while I smelled Gordon's hair. Right away, my cock stiffened in my jeans and I wondered if he could feel it pressing against him. I let one hand drift down to his ass and I squeezed a cheek, then I left my hand there, resting on his haunch.

Bringing his lips to my neck, he kissed me beneath my ear. "You slow dance nice, Beau-Beau; I like this much better."

My pulse pounded in my temples. *I can't believe this is happening.*

Without warning, Gordon shoved his hand down the front of my jeans. Seizing my cock in his fingers he said, "Somebody's stiff."

I turned my face to his and brought my mouth to Gordon's and we tongue-kissed, our chin stubbles scratching while Gordon squeezed my cock and toyed with the glans. We continued swaying in time with the music and my heart raced while I probed Gordon's mouth with my tongue, our lips smacking. I slid my hand inside the seat of his jeans and teased his asscrack with a finger.

Gordon chuckled deep in his throat, then he pulled his

lips from mine and looked at me. "So," he said, flickering his eyebrows, "do I have to sleep on the sofa tonight?"

On my bedroom bureau a candle flame danced. Otherwise, the cottage was dark as a tomb. Gordon and I undressed each other, each of us taking his time, starting with socks, then removing shirts. I sat on the edge of the double bed and Gordon stood before me. He was slim but sinewy, with a defined chest and dime-size nipples dark as raisins. I sucked them hard while Gordon groaned and ran his fingers through my hair. Candlelight reflected off a gold cross he wore on a chain hanging from his neck.

I tickled the line of fuzz descending from his navel, then I popped the button at his waist and lowered his zipper. Parting the flaps of his jeans, I shucked them to his ankles. He kicked them aside and his cock bulged in his white briefs, a damp spot appearing where the glans leaked precome. I reached for it, but Gordon swatted my hand away.

When I looked up, he waggled his eyebrows. "Not yet, Beau-Beau. I'm pantsing *you* first."

Blood rushed to my cheeks while I dropped my gaze and a smile crept onto my lips. "Okay," I said, standing.

Gordon got on his knees before me and opened up my jeans. My cock was rigid against my belly, the tip poking out my boxers' waistband. Gordon licked his lips; he lowered my jeans and helped me out of them. He still wore his ball cap, turned backward, and I thought he looked awfully sexy on his knees. He reached for the head of my cock and dipped his finger into a pearl of precome oozing from the slit. Bringing the finger to his tongue, he lapped my juice.

"Salty," he whispered, waggling his eyebrows.

His fingers stole inside the waistband of my boxers; he peeled them south and now I was naked, my cock bobbing before me. Gordon grabbed my asscheeks and pulled me to him. He nuzzled my pubic bush, then he licked my nuts while I groaned and played with his ears. How good it felt, being intimate with another man, especially one as cute as Gordon.

I thought, *This never would have happened if that storm hadn't come along. Our meeting was total happenstance.*

He seized the head of my cock in his fingers and lowered it from my belly. Shaking his head, he looked up at me and said, "You've got a whopper here, Beau-Beau. Want to fuck me with it?"

I nodded. Shoving my hands in his armpits, I pulled Gordon to his feet, then I yanked his briefs down and his genitals exploded into view, his cock bobbing like a diving board someone had leapt from. When he stepped out of his underwear I told him to hang them on the doorknob.

"I'll decide when you get them back," I said, grinning. "It might not be till Sunday."

His buttocks jiggled as he crossed the room to the door. When he turned back to me his eyes looked glittery, like he was high on some illegal drug.

"You plan on keeping me naked tomorrow, Beau-Beau?"

"I might," I said. "You look good in your birthday suit."

We fell to the bed, our chests meeting, cocks rubbing while we tongue-kissed and our lips smacked in the otherwise silent room. After a few minutes, Gordon pulled his mouth from mine. Our gazes met while he stroked my temple.

He said, "I knew you wanted me, the first night I came here."

"How?"

He snickered. "You should have seen your face when I took off the robe. It got so pale I thought you might pass out."

I blushed. Had I been *that* obvious?

"I've been waiting for you to make a move," Gordon said.

I squinted and asked, "Why didn't *you*?"

He raised a shoulder. "I'm a chickenshit, I guess. Afraid of rejection."

I took both our cocks in my fist and squeezed. "You don't have to worry about that with me. I'm yours for the rest of the summer if you'd like."

He made a little smile and nodded. "That sounds nice," he said.

Minutes later, after a bit of mutual fellatio, I rolled a condom onto my cock while Gordon lay on his back. He held his legs aloft, arms wrapped about his knees, exposing his pucker. I greased it with lube using one finger, then two. Then I brought the head of my cock to his hole and nudged.

"Easy," he whispered, "it's been a while."

"How long?" Already I felt jealous.

"Close to a year."

I eased inside him and he winced, sucking air through clenched teeth. "Jesus, you're big."

"You okay?"

He nodded, taking deep breaths while his hole flexed against the shaft of my cock, sending waves of pleasure through my limbs. How good it felt to gaze into his dark eyes, knowing I'd pierced his most private orifice.

Clearing his throat, he said, "Go on, Beau-Beau: fuck me."

I rode him hard, my nuts swinging, hips slapping his asscheeks while the bedsprings sang and the headboard drummed the wall. We both sweated and our bodies reflected candlelight. Gordon's milky skin was warm and smooth, and I thrilled to the movement of his muscles as I thrust inside him. I pinched his nipples till he groaned, then I bit his neck where it curved toward his shoulder. His sweat smelled like sweet milk, his hair like freshly mown grass.

Gordon used his fist to work his foreskin while I plunged inside him. "Jesus, this feels good," he told me, lips parting into a grin, teeth glistening. Each time I thrust he grunted.

I came first, a hoarse cry leaving my throat and bouncing off the walls. My body jerked each time I shot while sweat dripped from the tip of my nose and fell onto Gordon's chest. My orgasm completely overwhelmed me. My vision blurred and I thought I might faint.

When he spewed, Gordon cried my name while his come struck the headboard, the pillow beneath his head, then his chest, in a series of healthy spurts. His jizz looked like pearls, glistening in the candlelight. The stuff on the headboard oozed down into Gordon's hair. His lungs pumped like he'd just run a race and, I swear, I heard his heart thumping. I dipped a finger into a puddle of come near his collarbone, then I stuck the goo on my tongue. It tasted bitter, but in a good way, and after I swallowed I reached for more, hungry for his seed.

I stayed inside Gordon while our breathing relaxed and our pulses slowed. His pucker continued to flex, a love muscle caressing me.

He looked up and stroked my cheek. "That was...amazing, Beau-Beau."

I nodded, my gaze fixed on his. His eyes were luminous, so dark and beautiful, pools I could easily drown in. I stroked his sooty eyebrows with my thumb, then I kissed the tip of his needle nose.

He fingered the spot where I'd bit him. "Do I have a hickey?"

I bobbed my chin. The size of a postage stamp, it had already turned maroon in color.

He rolled his eyes. "How will I explain *that* to my folks?"

"You'll think of something. Tell them a dog bit you."

He giggled. "A dog *did* bite me: a sexy beast with a big dick."

I shifted my hips, still inside him and stiff as a broom handle. "Will you stay the rest of the weekend?"

Gordon nodded, running his fingers through my hair.

"Sure," he said, "I can do that."

We spent our Saturday naked.

Waking at dawn, we made love while sunlight slanted into the room through the eastern windows. The sex was even better than the night before, since we were sober now and entirely alert. Afterward, we showered, then I cooked breakfast: bacon and eggs, toast and orange juice. Gordon insisted on cleaning the kitchen, telling me, "I believe in fifty-fifty."

I sat on the sofa, reading a Doctorow novel, *Loon Lake*, and after he finished the dishes Gordon joined me, stretching out and resting his head in my lap. He read from Hemingway's collection, *The Nick Adams Stories*. I felt relaxed and contented, like I'd known Gordon all my life. Once in a while I'd run my fingers through his hair, fiddle with his nipple or finger his cock. I loved touching him like this, as though he were treasure I'd discovered. Occasionally he'd stroke my forearm or kiss my knuckles. His chest rose and fell as he breathed and I told myself, *I could stay here on this couch with Gordon for the rest of my life; I really could.*

The day was warm and bright. After lunch, we skinny-dipped in the lake, then lay on the dock, sunning ourselves, covering up with towels only when a boat passed by. Our mutual nudity bound us together; it made us comrades, gave the weekend a special and intimate feel.

The temperature plunged when the sun dropped behind the tree line. I stacked logs in our fireplace, then I got a blaze going and the two of us sat on a blanket before the hearth, watching flames dance while we sipped beer, our arms wrapped around each other's shoulders. Gordon talked about his childhood. He'd grown up in Camden, a coastal Maine town I'd visited several times, a picturesque place with a harbor full of sailboats and tree-lined streets where Cape Cods and brick colonials stood among emerald lawns.

"I know it looks like a postcard," Gordon told me, "but folks there are nosy. I have a dozen aunts and uncles in Camden and scores of cousins. Everyone knows everyone, so you have no privacy, no secrets. Folks are conservative and family oriented; it's no place for a gay boy."

When I asked if he'd ever had a lover he shook his head. "In Portland, I've met several guys over the Internet. I've gone to their homes for sex, but that's all. I'll walk in the door and maybe we'll share a beer, then it's off to bed. As soon as the sex is over, I'm gone."

"That's it? Don't you want more?"

Gordon looked at me and knitted his eyebrows. "Of course I do. It's just..."

"What?"

"I've never met someone like you before. Understand?"

His remark made my belly flutter. I brought my lips to his cheek and kissed him, then I laid my head on his shoulder and we didn't speak again for the longest time.

It seemed we didn't need to.

Sunday evening—after I'd dropped Gordon off at O'Connor's—I drove the county road, headlights cutting through darkness, and I felt so lonely I wanted to cry. Back at my cottage, I walked into the living room and the place seemed empty and cheerless. It wasn't the same without Gordon's presence. I glanced at the sofa, the dinette and the kitchen sink. I peeked into the bedroom, then the bathroom, recalling acts Gordon and I had performed in these places, our conversations and our lovemaking. How special each moment had been. Why had the weekend ended so quickly?

I couldn't wait for Monday morning to come, so I could pick up Gordon and bring him to my place. We could have sex before commencing our work, right? I looked at the kitchen clock and it seemed as if the second hand *crept* along. Had someone poured syrup into the clock's movements?

I shook my head and my eyes itched anew.

Beau, I told myself, *I think you're in love.*

I woke to an overcast sky on Monday, and as I drove to O'Connor's I wondered if it might rain. If it did, Gordon and I would forgo installing roof shingles. The thought of spending the day inside with Gordon made my pulse quicken, my cock stir. I longed to hear Gordon's voice, to stroke his cheek.

I came upon a gaggle of moose, a half-dozen or so, the largest a male with enormous antlers. They stood in the middle of the road, licking the asphalt, oblivious to my presence, and I had to drive onto the road shoulder to get past them. I shook my head and chuckled. *Only in Maine....*

At O'Connor's, Gordon wasn't waiting for me outside the camp's office, so I parked the truck and waited, listening to the radio and chewing a hangnail. Ten minutes passed and still Gordon did not appear, and then a bearlike man in a ball cap and flannel shirt emerged from the office, hitching his work pants. Lumbering to the passenger door of my truck, he stuck his head through the open window.

"Are you James Beauregard?"

I nodded.

He handed me an envelope. "Gordon Noyle left this for you."

"He's not here?"

The man shook his head. "Gordon settled his bill last night. This morning he put his boat on a trailer and left before daybreak."

I thought, *Trailer? I thought Gordon didn't own a car.*

I said, "What about Gordon's folks? What about his brothers and sisters? Did they all leave too?"

The man looked at me like I was daft. He said, "Noyle was here alone."

A shiver ran through me while the man walked away.

Inside the envelope was a single sheet of spiral notebook paper. I fingered its crinkly edge while I studied Gordon's blocky handwriting.

> Beau:
>
> My mom's diabetic and she's felt poorly the last few days. This morning her blood sugar level is seriously out of control, so we must take her to the hospital in Camden. I have no idea when or if we'll return to O'Connor's. It all depends.
>
> I enjoyed the weekend at your place, more than you know. Sorry to have to say good-bye this way.
>
> *Gordon.*

I felt like someone had punched me in the stomach. For a moment I thought I might puke. Gordon was gone? Just like that?

Driving home, a tear rolled from the corner of my eye. Last night I'd assumed I would see Gordon every day for the next few weeks. I'd savor his presence as we worked, and each afternoon we'd make love. Weekends we'd fish or take hikes in the woods, and maybe we'd visit Greenville for a lobster dinner.

But no.

None of it would happen, would it?

I pulled onto the gravel road leading to my cottage and braked. Shifting into park, I thrust my face into my hands and wept like a five-year-old.

Why was life so unfair?

Three days after Gordon's departure I was going crazy. I'd lost my appetite, and even *looking* at food made me nauseous. I slept poorly and performed no work on the cottage. All I wanted to do was drink alcohol. My dad kept a few liquor bottles in a cupboard, and one evening I drank rum and colas till I puked. Next morning I woke on the sofa, still fully dressed, my head pounding.

You can't keep this up, Beau. Pull yourself together.

What could I do? I *had* to see Gordon. I needed to hear him tell me he cared for me as much as I cared for him. But how could I find him? I didn't have his Camden phone number or address. Undressing, I dragged myself into the shower, then I let warm water pound my shoulders while I pondered what I should do next.

Camden's not a long drive, less than two hours. Go down there and find Gordon.

Tell him you love him.

I'd forgotten how pretty Camden was: the tree-lined streets, the stately homes with hedges trimmed just so, the quaint shops and restaurants. When I was ten my family had taken a windjammer cruise out of Camden's harbor on a ninety-foot, wooden sailing vessel called *Scud*. Built in the 1880s, *Scud's* hull was painted forest green. Its main mast was as big around as an oil barrel, probably thirty feet tall. For three days we cruised the coastline and even now I recalled details of the trip: rocky points thrusting into the sea, the birds and sunsets, whales and seals and brine-scented air.

Now I stood in a phone booth, leafing through pages of the Camden directory. I didn't know Gordon's father's first name, and there must have been two dozen Noyles listed. What should I do? Call each number and ask for Gordon? How much sense did *that* make?

Then I recalled Gordon had told me his father did construction work. Turning to the yellow pages, I looked under *Building Contractor* and, yes, there was a listing for *Noyle Construction.*

My hand shook as I dialed the number, then I cursed when an automated service answered my call. I didn't even bother to leave a message. What would I say? "Hi, I'm Gordon's boyfriend and I need to see him?"

I drummed my fingers against the phone booth's glass pane. All around me, tourists in shorts and tennis shoes strolled in the sunshine, many licking ice-cream cones, smiles painting their faces. Little kids darted here and there, knees chugging. Shops around the harbor did a brisk business, selling nautical paraphernalia, moose T-shirts, miniature sailing ships in bottles, sea captains and lighthouses carved from wood, watercolors depicting Maine's rocky coast.

Leaving the phone booth, I strode down a crowded sidewalk, hands in my pockets, my gaze fixed on the pavement as I tried to concentrate. A construction crew performed demolition work inside a storefront, a group of guys dressed in overalls and work boots. They used crowbars and sledgehammers to dismantle room partitions, and two were close to Gordon's age. Sticking my head in the door, I asked one if he knew Gordon Noyle.

He shook his head. "Is he local?"

I nodded.

"We're all from Freeport," he told me. "Sorry."

I wrenched my lips, feeling frustrated and discouraged, but a few minutes later I came upon a café with NOYLE'S BREAKFAST & LUNCH painted on the plate-glass window. The place was crowded with patrons seated at Formica-topped tables, perusing menus or chewing sandwiches; it smelled of frying bacon and coffee. I took a seat at the counter, and a waitress in a mint-green uniform, who looked maybe thirty, offered me a menu.

I said, "Just a glass of cola with ice, please."

When she brought my drink, I asked her if she knew Gordon, and my heart skipped a beat when she nodded.

"He's my cousin," she said.

"I'm a friend. I'm passing through Camden and I thought I'd say hi, but I don't have Gordon's address or phone number."

She glanced at her wristwatch. "He's likely at the church this time of day."

"Church?"

She nodded. "St. Catherine's on Baxter Avenue. It's the tallest steeple in town; you can't miss it."

I crinkled my nose and squinted. Why would Gordon be at a church on a Wednesday afternoon?

St. Catherine's was a brick structure with stained glass windows and a pair of coffered entry doors. A sign in the manicured lawn announced that Vacation Bible School—grades one through six—was in session, June first through the end of August.

Gordon stood in a playground surrounded by a chain-link fence. Three dozen children clambered on jungle gyms, rode swings and played four-square on a cement court. One child, a little boy perhaps seven, leaned against Gordon while Gordon's arm rested on the boy's shoulders. The boy rubbed the tip of his nose while Gordon spoke to him.

Gordon wore a black shirt, a white priest's collar, black pants and shoes that looked to be patent leather, also black.

My stomach churned and my vision blurred. What was going on?

I crossed the church's emerald lawn, approaching the chain-length fence, and Gordon didn't sense my presence until I spoke his name. When I did he swung his gaze to me and his eyebrows arched.

Bending at the waist, Gordon spoke to the little boy, who scooted toward a seesaw while Gordon walked toward me, arms swinging, his mouth a thin line. My heart fluttered when he drew near because he looked so handsome in his dark clothing.

How badly I'd missed him. I wanted to kiss Gordon, right there in front of the kids.

Gordon placed his hands on top of the fence. Puckering one side of his face, he said, "Surprise, Beau," then he brought an index finger to his chest. "Meet the *real* Gordon Noyle."

My knees turned to jelly and my voice cracked when I spoke. "Everything you told me about yourself was a...lie?"

"Not all, but some."

"Why?"

He shrugged. "I have an alter ego. He emerges when I meet an attractive man outside of Camden. Understand?"

I shook my head.

Gordon looked here and there, then he whispered, "That first night at your cottage, I wanted you and I knew you wanted me. But honestly, Beau-Beau, would we have made love if you'd known I was a priest?"

I studied my shoes and didn't say anything. The kids' piping voices grated on my nerves, and I fought an urge to turn and run to my truck.

It was all false. Gordon's a fraud.

My eyes watered. I looked at Gordon and asked him, "Did it mean anything to you? The time we spent together?"

Gordon glanced over his shoulder at the kids, then returned his gaze to me. "Of course it did, Beau. I like you so much; you're handsome and sweet and having sex with you was wonderful."

I rubbed my eyes with the heels of my hands and sniffled.

"You deserve someone better," Gordon said, "a person who's truthful and not afraid to be himself."

I wanted to tell Gordon it was okay; that I'd overlook his deceit if he'd only come back to First Roach Pond, but before I could speak a girl with a mop of auburn hair and freckles on her nose approached. "Father Noyle," she said, "I skinned my knee. Do you have a bandage?"

A trickle of blood, shiny as nail polish, oozed down the girl's bumpy shin.

Gordon looked at her wound, then at me.

"I have to go," he said.

A few days later, while Peter Demens, proprietor of Kokadjo's general store, rang up my purchases, he asked, "Did the fellow from Camden ever contact you?"

I said, "Excuse me?"

"The dark-haired young man."

"You mean Gordon?"

Peter shrugged. "He didn't tell me his name. You were leaving as he was coming into the store and he asked about you, said he was close to your age and he needed a fishing buddy."

A shiver ran up my spine.

I said, "How long ago was this?"

Peter scratched his head. "Must have been two weeks or so, just before that nasty storm. Remember how hard the wind blew?"

I nodded.

"Anyway, he seemed like a nice fellow, so I gave him directions to your place. You never heard from him?"

The second week of August, I stood shirtless on a ladder, painting trim on the cottage's eaves. Late morning sunshine warmed my shoulders. I heard an engine's mutter and the sound of tires crushing gravel, and when I looked toward the driveway a pickup truck approached, missing its front bumper.

The driver was Gordon Noyle.

After we shook his gaze traveled over the cottage. "Looks good," he said. "The new roof really dresses the place up."

"Listen," I said, "I never paid you for the work you did. Let me write you a check."

He raised a palm and shook his head. "Being with you was payment enough, Beau-Beau."

His remark made my knees wobble. My voice wavered when I asked him, "What brings you to the lake?"

He dropped his gaze and shoved his hands inside the back pockets of his blue jeans. Then he kicked dirt with the toe of his work boot. His flannel shirt was unbuttoned; the T-shirt beneath was faded and coffee-stained. He hadn't shaved in a few days, and he looked like a guy who worked at a sawmill instead of a Catholic priest from Camden.

He said, "I know you'll leave soon. I wanted to see you, to say I am sorry."

"It's all right, Gordon, I—"

He looked up. "No, it's not 'all right.' I'm such a...coward; I hate myself sometimes. I wasn't fair to you, and there's no excuse for it. Can you forgive me?"

I told him of course I could.

Gordon smiled wanly. "Thanks, Beau-Beau." He reached for

my paint-splattered chest. Fingering a nipple, he told me, "You look good with your shirt off."

My cock twitched.

I threw an arm about Gordon's neck and pulled him to me and our chests and hips met. Burying the tip of my nose in his hair, I inhaled its grassy scent.

"I've missed you so much," I said.

Minutes later we lay naked in my bed, Gordon's legs hiked, my hips thrusting, cock poking Gordon's prostate, making him squeal and grunt. The day was warm and we both sweated, and our skin stuck together as if we'd been glued. The bedsprings wheezed and the headboard drummed the wall behind it, as before.

When I flooded the condom with my seed I hollered like a lunatic while my heart thumped and my lungs heaved. I felt my orgasm in every part of my body, even in my scalp and the soles of my feet. How I'd missed this. How would I ever live without it?

Gordon worked his foreskin with a fist. He whispered, "Stay inside me, Beau-Beau; don't leave," and very soon his irises rolled up inside his head, then he spewed sticky pearls of semen onto his collarbone. Gordon's pucker flexed against the shaft of my cock; he shouted my name at the ceiling, his chest rising and falling, his breath huffing as though the room lacked oxygen.

I didn't withdraw for a while. Instead I held Gordon as tight as I could while our breathing relaxed and our pulses slowed. Outside the bedroom window a squirrel barked in a tree and the sound echoed through the woods.

Imagine, I thought, *doing this every day. Waking to Gordon each morning. Falling asleep in his arms at night.*

"Beau-Beau?"

"Yeah?"

Gordon ran his fingers through my hair. “That was wonderful.”

“It certainly was.”

“So, tell me about Florida. What’s it like?”

“Your nose is sunburned,” I tell Gordon.

“I can’t help it,” he says. “The beach is so beautiful I could walk it forever.”

I sit on our screened porch, grading students’ vocabulary tests on a Saturday morning. The sun ascends in a cloudless sky and the day is warming up. Gordon’s hair is damp and his skin smells of salt water as he approaches and kisses my cheek. He wears bathing trunks and rubber sandals and he’s shirtless, looking so sexy my cock stirs at the sight of his slender physique.

Our cottage isn’t much: a one bedroom with a galley kitchen, a bath with a shower stall, pedestal sink and john. But it’s one block from a beach with emerald water and sand white as table sugar. Every evening we stroll down there to watch the sunset. The sky boils with shades of pink, green and gold, and the sound of waves smacking the shore mixes with seabird cries.

It has been eight months since I met Gordon at First Roach Pond, and much has changed. Six months back, Gordon left Camden and the priesthood. When he told his parents about us, and how he planned to live with me in Florida, they became upset. Cruel things were said, threats made, and for many months Gordon did not speak with his family.

Then, one afternoon when I returned home from school, Gordon’s mom, Stephanie, called from Maine, and we spoke for almost an hour. I told her I loved Gordon and he loved me and I said things were fine. We were happy, I said.

Now, things seem okay between Gordon and his folks. He talks with them every Sunday evening, and they plan to visit

Florida in June, once Gordon's five siblings are released from school for the summer. We'll meet them at Disney World for a couple of days, then they'll rent a hotel room near our place and we'll all get better acquainted.

When people truly love one another things have a way of working out, don't they?

Gordon waits tables at a chain restaurant, five nights a week. The tips are good and the manager likes Gordon, and there's talk of a promotion in the near future. Gordon has joined a chapter of Dignity, the church for gay and lesbian Catholics. It's not sanctioned by Rome, of course, but Gordon says that doesn't matter. He knows God loves him, he says. Once a month he'll conduct mass and I'll attend, to see Gordon in his vestments and hear his sermon. He's a good speaker; people like him and they pay attention to what he says.

I'm so proud of Gordon.

Now, I slip a finger inside the waistband of his swim trunks; I look up and ask him, "Headed for the shower?"

He nods.

"Mind if I join you?"

A grin spreads across Gordon's face and his eyes gleam like gemstones.

While warm water flows over us, I use soap for lubricant, and Gordon groans when I enter him from behind. I do a reach-around, gripping his rigid cock in my soapy fist and stroking while I thrust inside him. When I reach orgasm my cock throbs deep within Gordon, and he sprays the tiles before him with his seed.

"Feel good?" I say as our pulses slow.

"Mmm-hmmm."

"Do you love me?"

"Yeah, Beau-Beau, I do."

I ease my cock out of Gordon and it makes a popping sound, exiting his pucker. I seize his shoulders and turn him so he faces me. While water streams over us and gurgles in the drain, I kiss Gordon, then I say, "I want to know something."

He looks at me, eyebrows gathered. "What?"

"That night I first met you wasn't by chance, was it?"

He drops his gaze and a smile plays on his lips, then he looks at me again.

He says, "What do you think?"

"I think it was crazy, crossing First Roach Pond in that storm."

He shrugs and says, "Aren't you glad I did?"

Like I said, I don't believe in serendipity.

Sometimes a guy wants something so badly he'll do whatever is necessary to get it, like risking his life in a storm and maybe losing everything he's worked for: his job and his family.

All things happen for a reason, don't they?

BAXTER'S SAPFU

David Holly

How'd it go, Zef?" That was Baxter's typical way of starting a telephone conversation. No "Hello"—just jump right to the shit.

"FUBB," I said.

"FUBB? Not SUSFU or SNAFU?"

For the record, Baxter and I loved using the colorful acronyms of Army slang: SNAFU—situation normal, all fucked-up; FUBAR—fucked-up beyond all recognition; FUBB—fucked-up beyond belief; FUMTU—fucked-up more than usual; SAPFU—surpassing all previous fuck-ups; SUSFU—situation unchanged, still fucked-up; and TARFU—things are *really* fucked-up. To name a few.

"No, it was FUBB. I'm trying to decide between throwing myself off the tallest building in town or joining a monastery."

"You might get lucky in the monastery," Baxter said. "Those monks are horny buggers."

"Screw the monks. You slammed me with another failure, Baxter."

"Get the fuck out. You better tell me about it. Meet you at Ponce's in thirty?"

"What the fuck." It was a surprisingly warm April evening, and the next day was Sunday, so we could get soused without having to worry about sucking mints at the PTA meeting. Baxter was a social studies teacher at Millard Fillmore High School, where I taught English. Having discovered we were both gay but utterly incompatible as lovers, we became close confidantes.

I pulled on my bicycle shorts and jersey, checked the lights on my bicycle and mounted it. Twenty minutes later, I locked my bike to the rack outside Ponce's. Baxter was already seated at a table, two Peppermint Patty cocktails in front of him. Ponce's is the only bar in town swishy enough to serve Peppermint Patties.

Baxter pushed my drink toward me. His eyes twinkled with glee as he invited me to tell all. "Come on, Zef, how'd you manage to fuck up this date?"

I moaned. I took a sip from my Peppermint Patty, but it wasn't enough to ease my aching soul. "Len was gorgeous, like you said. Only problem—he wasn't thirty-two like you said. He couldn't have been a day over twenty. I felt like I was dating one of my high school boys."

"Not exactly a bad fantasy," Baxter said, signaling the waiter and ordering two more cocktails. "Except they'd put you in prison just for thinking it, and the line of stud cons, swinging dicks and horny old lags waiting to gangbang your ass would stretch around the whole cell block."

Ignoring Baxter's fantasies, I continued: "Len picked me up at my place and took me to FishCats. Seafood, right. So we're eating and all of a sudden, Len reaches out with his napkin and wipes my face. Seems I had tartar sauce running down my chin."

Baxter giggled and tried to spin a joke about cum facials, but

I interrupted him. "I felt like I was his old grandpa, drooling into my oatmeal."

"Is that all? That's what you call fucked-up beyond belief, Zef?"

"Oh, the tartar sauce was nothing but a SNAFU. You know how FishCats has that step up before you reach the host's desk?"

"Sure."

I emptied my glass before I spoke. "So I tripped."

"Oh, that's just FUMTU."

"Baxter, I sprawled. I fell flat on my face, and when I hit there was a loud ripping sound."

"You tore your pants?" Baxter gesticulated wildly to the waiter and held up four fingers. Four empty glasses sat in front of us, and Baxter was going for replacements wholesale.

"No, worse."

"Huh."

"For a second I didn't realize what had happened. Everyone in the restaurant was looking at me. Then I knew. When I hit the floor, I farted. Really loud. The whole restaurant heard me. FUBB."

Baxter could only gape in amazement. "How'd the date go after that?" he inquired at last.

I grabbed a glass from the waiter's hand and gulped the contents. "Len dropped me off at my house. Not even a good-night kiss. He said 'so long' and had driven halfway down the block before I reached my front door."

"Okay, that was FUBB."

"No shit."

"Len was the wrong guy for you, Zef," Baxter pronounced. "I can see that now."

"But you're the asshole who set me up for this failure," I protested. "You should have told me the truth to begin with." I drank another cocktail, vaguely wondering whether it was my fourth or fifth. I was feeling rather less inhibited.

Baxter shrugged. "No big deal, Zef. I met a guy last night who's perfect for you. I'll set it up."

"Don't bother, Baxter. Based upon past experience, he'd turn out to be seventy and weigh four hundred pounds."

A look of doubt flickered across Baxter's face. "Well, perhaps Ralph is a tad older. And I guess he could shed a pound or two." He shrugged and ordered several more rounds.

"Look, Baxter. I know you mean well. But as a matchmaker, you're FUBAR personified. I have to find my own boyfriends." I was feeling quite drunk. I leaned toward Baxter and spoke confidentially: "Another problem was that Len kept talking like he was into oral action exclusively. Blow jobs are okay, but they're not my first love. So even if I had hit it off with Len, he would not have delivered what I want."

So we left any future dates hanging, and I set about trying to find my own boyfriends. Three months passed without a single guy sharing my bed. Then, out of the blue, as I was preparing to swim laps in the gym pool, my world changed.

I had bought my new turquoise swim briefs online. Checking out my assets in the mirror, I decided that the garment fit a bit too tight to be truly attractive. Mother Nature had gifted me with a bountiful bubble butt, so finding a bikini that covered my ass comfortably was a challenge.

"Looking tight, Mr. Wells," a voice hailed.

A chill gripped my groin. The compliment had come from one of my high school students. Stung by the suggestive sarcasm, I muttered, "Tend to your studies, Julio."

"We're on vacation," Julio called as I padded toward the swimming pool. Running into a student, especially a wiseass like Julio, inhibited my strut and left me self-conscious.

Sometimes a fellow can be plodding along completely self-absorbed when something happens that is so startling it tosses him for a loop. Miracles happen when we least expect them. Walking along the edge of the pool, I spied a gorgeous man gliding through the blue water of the second lane. Practicing a dolphin kick, he humped his ass down the lane. I could not tear my eyes from him. Wearing sexy swim briefs with a rear seam that streamlined his butt, he slithered through the water with an enticing swish.

I was so engrossed that I tripped over some damned fool's discarded flip-flops, toppled sideways, and *kerplopped* into the hot tub with an almighty splash. For a second I must have been disoriented because I came to myself on the edge of the tub with the gorgeous swimmer pressing his lips to mine. He pumped my chest and blew air into my mouth with such tenderness that I wanted to die just so he could resurrect me.

"Hi," I breathed, staring into his liquid eyes.

"Welcome back," he said. "I was afraid that you'd passed into Summerland."

I didn't know what he meant about *passing into Summerland*, but I was glad that I hadn't passed gas. "What is Summerland?" I asked.

"The afterlife," he said smiling, "where you dwell in eternal youth with those people, pets and things you cherished."

"Maybe you should give me more mouth-to-mouth resuscitation," I suggested. A titter of juvenile laughter met that remark. Rising to a seated position, I saw that Julio was sitting in the hot tub.

My savior gave Julio a firm look. "It's not funny. Your boyfriend nearly drowned." That comment nearly caused Julio to drown.

"I wish he was my boyfriend," Julio gasped.

"Julio was one of my high school students," I informed my savior. "In my British literature class this past school year." His eyes widened at that. "Not what you're thinking. I didn't even know he was a member of this club until I ran into him in the locker room a few minutes ago."

Julio grinned obscenely at me and climbed out of the hot tub. My former student was radiantly attired in a tropical floral-patterned thong swimsuit. His tanned derrière stuck out provocatively, and the front pouch was well filled.

My eyes must have bugged out as I stared at Julio's enticing rump. For his part, my student wiggled his ass as he sauntered toward the sauna. My savior took me gently by the arm. "I'm Aeslin. Aeslin Blackthorne."

"Zef Wells."

"Zef?"

I colored. "Short for Zephyr."

Aeslin gave me a bright look. "That's quite the pagan name. Are you a pagan?"

"Uh, not to speak of. I'm not sure I'm anything. Religiously, that is."

"I belong to a gay Wiccan circle. The Coven of the Magical Men. Would you like to attend a meeting with me?"

"Is that allowed? Bringing in outsiders, I mean?"

"Sure."

"I'd like to come, too." Instead of going into the sauna, Julio had been eavesdropping. "I'm gay. And Mr. Wells is my hero."

For the first time, I realized that Julio had not been mocking me. This sixteen-year-old high school boy had a crush on me. A revolting sense of responsibility descended. I wanted to encourage him to accept his sexuality while discouraging him from forming an attachment to me. Furthermore, I had to be the gay role model, and no way did I feel like being any boy's hero, much less the hero of a swishy Latino teenager with solid buttocks cut by his sexy swim thong.

"I doubt they'd allow underage lads, Julio," I began, but Aeslin interrupted me.

"Of course you can participate in a circle, Julio," he said. Aeslin smiled at me. "Wicca isn't a sex club," he said. "A circle isn't a gay bathhouse. Attending a pagan ritual with a student present is no different from attending the same church, synagogue, temple or mosque."

Not in the eyes of the school board, I thought, but I withheld my doubts.

Aeslin, Julio and I swam laps down the fitness club's pool until we were gasping. Watching Julio's butt slide above the surface of the pool was disturbing, but seeing Aeslin's gorgeous derrière break surface was a delicacy to behold.

"Zef, would you have lunch with me?" Aeslin asked as we lounged in the hot tub to warm our muscles after the cool, salty pool water.

"I'm hungry," Julio offered before I could respond.

Aeslin gave me a querying look. I winked at him, showing more assurance than I felt. "Julio," I said, trying to broach the subject gently. "Aeslin is asking me on a date. Yes, I want you to be proud and out, but..."

"You don't want me horning in on your date," Julio interrupted with a snort. "Sure as shit, you want his cock, and three makes a crowd. I'd rather make it a threesome, Mr. Wells, but I get it. The principal would crucify you during ninth period assembly if you let me slide my cock up your sweet ass. I'm jailbait on the hoof, fuck it all."

"Shit, Julio," I swore, aghast that he had divined my proclivities. "You're just sixteen, and a high school student."

"*No problemo, mi hermano*," Julio said. "But just you wait

two years, Mr. Wells. Just you wait and see."

"Maybe."

"Maybe, hell. I'm grown enough, and I want your body. My dick gets hard. I jerk off. And whatever the principal and school board think, when I stroke my cock I think about your cute ass. How about that, Mr. Wells!"

I don't know what I would have done had Aeslin not begun laughing. "You're right, Julio," he gasped amid sidesplitting gales. "Zef does have a cute ass."

"I know a great little seafood place," Aeslin said after we had changed into our street clothes and he had programmed Julio's phone number and promised to call about the circle gathering.

Aeslin had a green Honda Element. I had bicycled to the gym, so we pushed my bike into the back of his car. We chatted as we drove along, and I asked him what he did for a living.

"I make costumes."

"You sew?"

"Oh, yes. I own a costume shop. I sell my creations at renaissance fairs, festivals, science fiction and fantasy conventions, and the like. I even make my own clothes. Someday I hope to switch from costumes to fashion. Maybe compete on 'Project Runway.'"

I had noticed that his clothing fit him exquisitely. "Did you make your swimsuit?"

Aeslin grinned knowingly. "Want me to make you one like it?"

I'd known him for less than two hours, and he was ready to measure my ass for swim briefs. "Yeah, sure," I gasped.

"Okay," he said. "After lunch, I'll run a tape measure over your butt."

The town must have boasted fifty seafood restaurants, but I

was not surprised when we parked at FishCats. My crowd always ended up at FishCats. Surprisingly enough, I made it through the meal with Aeslin without dribbling tartar sauce, falling down or ripping out a fart. Our conversation was interesting, if offbeat. Aeslin explained the Wiccan way to me. Gripping my hand, he fastened his glistering eyes on me and intoned:

"'Keep pure your ideal, strive ever toward it, for mine is the secret door unto the land of youth, and mine is the cup of the wine of life, the grail of immortality.'"

"That's the Wiccan Rede?" I asked.

"No," he breathed, "that's from the Charge of the Great Goddess." Aeslin drew a deep breath. "The Rede is 'an ye harm none, do as thou wilt.'"

"A Wiccan can do anything he wants? Anything?"

"Just so long as he does no harm."

I was intrigued. Aeslin was sincere and charming, and his religion—if it could be called a religion—sounded innocuous. More than innocuous, his magical circle enticed me.

"I'd like to attend one of your circles."

"Sooner than you think, Zef."

"You also promised Julio. Let's be careful. He's sixteen, and remember, he was one of my students."

"I understand, Zef. But Julio asked, and asking is the first step toward freedom."

I didn't know what to say to that comment. Aeslin seemed to be sincere about his less-than-traditional beliefs, and I then knew nothing about the Wiccan religion beyond the humbug strewn by mainstream religions that warred against other faiths or viewed them as competitors to be crushed.

Our lunch finished, I rode with Aeslin to his shop. The front windows of his storefront seemed small contrasted with the miraculously spacious interior. I could scarcely believe the amount of merchandise offered for sale: everything from hand-sewn kilts to harlequin tights, brilliant thongs to feathered trousers graced the bodies of mannequins.

An attractive blonde dressed as Pocahontas was standing behind the cash register. "This is Sal Dent." Aeslin waved his hand toward the blonde. "My cousin."

"Merry meet, Zef," Sal said.

A guy in a skintight, anatomically detailed Cowardly Lion suit spun on his Rollerbladed feet. "And her brother Al." Al waved with one hand as he wheeled and hung a collection of sparkling shirts on a rack.

Curling an arm around my waist, Aeslin led me up a flight of stairs to the studio. This designing, cutting and sewing room occupied the entire floor. Bolts of fabric by the hundreds leaned against the walls. Aeslin grabbed a tape measure. "Get undressed."

I hastened to comply. No sooner had I dropped my shorts than he slipped the tape measure around my buttocks. He grabbed a bolt of nylon-Lycra with a tropical sunset print, measured briefly and cut pieces from the fabric.

I watched with fascination as he sewed the pieces together, inserting elastic for the waistband, leg openings and rear seam. I could scarcely believe how fast and accurately he worked. Within fifteen minutes, he had turned out a splashy swim garment.

Grinning proudly, he said, "Raise your leg." I raised my right leg, and he slipped the swim briefs over my foot. I stepped into them with my left, and Aeslin pulled them up, adjusted my cock and balls in the front pouch, and aligned the rear seam. "Take a look, Zef," he said, pulling me toward a full-length mirror.

The swim briefs held hints of red, orange, purple and even a flash of green, the colors of the sun setting off the West Indies.

The pouch accentuated my maleness while the rear seam celebrated my anal cleft.

"You look good enough to fuck," Aeslin joked. I wiped the grin off his face by touching my lips to his. Our mouths pressed and I snuggled closer. His heat warmed my body. My swimsuit tightened as I slid my tongue over his lips. I licked his teeth, and then I met his tongue. His hand slid down my back, exploring my bare skin. Revealed in all my hot lust, I felt naked beside him.

I gripped his solid butt through his trousers, kissing him harder. A low moan rumbled through him, and it seemed to originate not just with his mouth, but with his lungs and heart. His hand gripped my ass, and his fingers slid into my crack.

"Aeslin, did you order the ivory linen for the boatman's shirts?" Sal Dent yelled, entering the studio. Then she emitted a gasp. "Whoops, blessed be, boys," she said with a giggle.

"What's going on?" Al inquired, completing our audience. "Hot shit, Aeslin. He's gonna stretch that swimsuit all out of shape."

My erection deflated then, and I stood rather abashed. "Don't be embarrassed, Zef," Aeslin said. "My cousins are pagans too. We all worship sex."

"Hot gay man-to-man action pleases the goddess," Al said helpfully.

"Is that what you do in your rituals?"

"Not at all," Sal said. "The great rite is reserved for a special purpose."

"The moon is full tonight," Al said, giving Aeslin a suggestive look.

"He's hinting that I should invite you to the ritual," Aeslin said. "Will you attend with me?"

"Yes," I said, uttering the word that would change my life.

* * *

The house stood to the north of the city where the backyards were larger and more private. A high wooden fence surrounded this yard, and the thick hedge outside ensured privacy. Eight fellows of various ages were talking quietly when we drove up. Aeslin introduced me around, explaining that I was his guest. Al arrived just then. He hugged me and his cousin, but said nothing beyond "Merry meet."

We knocked on the wooden gate, and a man dressed in a light silvery cloak decorated with crimson symbols admitted us. Not surprisingly, the man who owned the house was also High Priest. He greeted each of us with a chaste kiss.

A shed had been converted to a comfortable changing room, including a bathroom with a large shower. We undressed and slipped crimson cloaks over our heads. The cloaks were light but the breeze was warm and the moon shone brightly upon the yard. As Aeslin led me to the sacred space, I felt a sense of wonder. Something that was neither a cold chill nor a hot flash rushed over me.

"It's the magic," Aeslin whispered. The priest anointed our foreheads with scented oil as we entered the circle. Once we were safely inside, he walked three times around with his wand, sealing our sacred ground. Then he invoked the watchtowers and banished any who would wish us harm.

A short ceremony, like a miracle play, followed, in which we learned of the deeds of the gay gods. Then we raised power to overcome the misfortunes that had befallen an absent member. The ceremony left me feeling as though I were walking with both feet in the air. When we sat to partake of ale, sweetened seed cakes and apple cider, I found that I was shaking. Aeslin placed his arm around me.

"I've never felt this way before."

"The feeling grows stronger with each ritual," Aeslin breathed.

"I want to be a part of this. To dwell in the magic always."

Smiling gaily, Aeslin whispered, "'And thou who thinkest to seek for me, know thy seeking and yearning shall avail thee not unless thou knowest the mystery; that if that which thou seekest thee findest not within thee, thou wilt never find it without thee. For behold, I have been with thee from the beginning; and I am that which is attained at the end of desire.'"

Two o'clock had slipped off the clock face before we returned to Aeslin's apartment on the third floor of his building, just above his design studio. His cousins had rooms there too. However, Al had gone off with a guy from our circle, and Sal had not yet returned home from her own gathering.

When the door shut behind us, Aeslin pulled me close. "You are so beautiful, Zef," he said. His hands played over my buttocks as we kissed. Right then I knew that he wanted my ass. Fortunately, my ass was one attribute that I was eager to give to him.

By morning we were largely satiated, both of us having come twice. I was stunned to see that we had slept until nearly eleven. Aeslin called down to the shop and spoke to Al. Assured that all was well, we played and groped each other as we fried apples with spices, baked a sweet corn bread, and whipped eggs with chives and grated parmesan cheese. We wrapped the omelets around the fried apples and sweetened our corn bread with melted butter and honey from a comb.

"Witchcraft!" Baxter shrieked into the phone. "FUBAR! FUBAR! FUBAR!"

Baxter was raised an evangelical Protestant, and he was still one at heart, no matter how many cocks he had sucked in his lifetime. I bit my tongue, regretful that I had told him about the magical ritual that changed my life. I finally pried myself off the phone and fled to the gym. Naturally, I ran into Julio in the weight room. Julio was turning heads in his liquid purple shorts and tapered shirt. My student promptly asked whether I "got lucky" with Aeslin.

I was in the middle of a squat when Julio called out, "Did you sit on his cock?" Heads turned.

"Julio, that's not a proper question for a student to ask his teacher," I admonished. I *had* sat on Aeslin's cock, but it was none of Julio's business.

Leaving the gym after my workout, I biked to Aeslin's shop. Sal Dent was stuffing a young man into a thong with a front chamois flap. She pointed toward the ceiling. "He's in the studio."

Aeslin was designing an exotic carnival costume. He was frowning at a handful of green feathers when I entered, but he threw them down and greeted me joyously. After a kiss that loosened my toenails, I told him about my conversation with Baxter.

Aeslin shook his head sadly. "Think about the burning times, Zef," he said. "The cruel prejudice against us has come down since the vandals tried to wipe out all knowledge of our religion, along with all who practiced the old ways."

Because I was on my summer break, my time was my own. However, the premier drag event, the Clandestine Ball, was fast approaching, and Aeslin was making clothes for the Colonial Court of the Queens of the Riding. I spent my afternoon assisting him in selecting feathers and sequins. I couldn't sew a stitch, but I've always had an eye for fashion. I'd like to think that I was more help than nuisance.

That evening we drove to the gym for a swim. I pulled up

my swim briefs and gasped at the way they gripped my flesh. When I had tried them on in Aeslin's studio, my unruly cock had distorted their fit. The rear seam conformed to my ass so well that I felt both better dressed and less dressed, and more comfortable, in that swimsuit than any other. Sashaying along the edge of the pool, I did not become aroused, but I could sense the arousal of others.

Aeslin and I plowed the pool side by side. The water flowed off my body, and I vowed never again to wear a swimsuit without a rear seam. The added definition shot my ass through the fluid with little resistance.

Back in Aeslin's suite, we cooked a light supper. We followed supper with an extended session of passionate kissing, followed by equally passionate lovemaking. We took a protracted shower after the sex. As Aeslin slid the bar of soap up my buttcrack and washed me with his hand, he whispered his love in my ear. "Yes, Aeslin, I believe that you do love me. And I love you." I had found my soul's mate, my other half.

In the late afternoon, I returned to my apartment to check my mail. Only then did I realize that my cell phone was sitting on the charger. I had been so preoccupied with Aeslin that I had forgotten it.

Fifteen voice mail messages awaited me. Half were from Baxter and the rest from phone numbers I did not recognize. I tried one of the unknown numbers and discovered that the call had come from the local newspaper. The next I tried was from a television news reporter. I hung up without stating my name.

When I got Baxter on the phone, he sounded contrite—quite unlike his usual demeanor. "SAPFU, Zef. I'm so sorry."

My heart leaped into my throat. What could Baxter have done that surpassed all his previous fuck-ups? The possibilities boggled the mind.

"I've got messages from reporters," I ventured. "What did you do?"

"Well, you saw the article." Baxter's voice sounded strangled.

A freezing sensation gripped my balls. "What fucking article?"

Baxter gulp sounded like he was swallowing a melon. "In today's paper."

The Northwest Bugle was sitting on my table, still in its orange wrapper. Setting down the phone—Baxter could hang fire for a few minutes—I began to leaf through it. The article was mercifully short, but I saw that it was barely the window dressing for the curtain of fire to follow.

Local Teacher Suspected of Witchcraft
by Bryce Dickens

An English teacher at Millard Fillmore High School is suspected of being a secret member of an all-male witches' coven.

Zephyr Wells, who teaches impressionable teenagers as young as fourteen, is an openly homosexual male.

Pastor John Tuttle of the Last Hope Baptist Church spoke with the Bugle *after a troubled parishioner sought counseling upon learning of Mr. Wells's affiliation with the secret cult.*

"Naturally, we are concerned," Pastor Tuttle said. "This man teaches minor children."

Tuttle clarified his concerns when he said, "How could this man not present a danger to our children?"

> *A perusal of Wiccan websites revealed images of bizarre ceremonies conducted in the nude.*
>
> *According to A. W. Pope of Christup.com, Wiccans claim to practice a nature-oriented religion, which raises speculation about fertility rituals, including orgiastic group sex.*
>
> *"Allowing perverts like Wells to enter a classroom is a violation of our child protection laws," Pastor Tuttle said.*
>
> *"We have a problem with witchcraft in our schools. Homosexual witches are indoctrinating our children into Satanic sexual perversions."*
>
> *Despite repeated phone calls from the* Bugle, *Mr. Wells could not be reached for comment.*

Calmly, I folded the paper and picked up the phone.

"Holy fucking ape shit, Baxter," I screamed. "I suppose that you were the asshole 'troubled parishioner' who sought counseling."

"I didn't realize that Pastor Tuttle would react so strongly," Baxter admitted.

Before my horrified eyes swept a vision of my new lover reading the newspaper. "Aeslin!" I shouted and dropped the phone. Forgetting Baxter, I rushed out the door and biked to the studio. Sal Dent was locking up when I arrived.

"Back so soon?" she grinned lewdly. "The cum factory must be working overtime."

"Did you read the newspaper?" I demanded, already halfway up the stairs.

"I'm over here," Aeslin called from behind a rack of ornate capes.

Wheeling on the stairs, I waved the newspaper at him. "It's a disaster," I cried. Without warning, I burst into tears.

Aeslin laid the paper aside and took me into his arms. "Nothing is that bad, Zef," he said. His smooth hands caressed my shoulders. He pulled me tighter against him.

Brokenly, I related what had happened. Sal picked up the paper and read the article aloud while Aeslin kissed away my tears. Our kisses grew more passionate as our bodies responded to each other. His hands wandered down my back until he gripped my buttocks.

"At a time like this," I asked, heedless that Sal would discover that I loved deep anal penetration, "you still want my ass?"

Hot lust swept over me as I said it, a desire so fiery that I could scarcely believe it. My career might lie in ashes, my community might shun me, my students might be mocking me, and I was about to deal with the situation by getting screwed in the best way. "I want you inside, Aeslin. I want your cum."

Preoccupied with the newspaper, Sal Dent yelped, "This is shit!" Then she chuckled, "But it's kinda funny."

Ignoring Sal, Aeslin and I slipped upstairs. As before, I started off taking the passive role, but as the night progressed we switched back and forth. Our lovemaking was richer than before, and our bond grew closer. Aeslin began to tell me about his life, his hippie parents who found his gayness "cool," the taunts and bullying he had endured in school and the path that led him into sewing and design.

I told him some of my secrets as well, and by morning I knew him better than I knew Baxter. "Do you feel like you should have known me all your life?" Aeslin asked.

It was a funny question, but I knew what he meant. It was like being reunited with a lost love, even though we had never met before that week.

* * *

The next morning, Aeslin, Sal, Al and I met around the table and planned our media strategy. We composed my statement, edited it, proofread it, revised it some more and practiced reading it aloud until every word rang with the clarity of absolute truth.

Finished, we hired a messenger service to hand deliver copies to the reporter Bryce Dickens, his editors and publishers. We also sent copies to every other paper in the region, even the weeklies and the shopper rags. Then I rang up the television news channels and scheduled a press conference for that afternoon.

Standing on the steps with Millard Fillmore High as my backdrop, I addressed the cameras and reporters: "My name is Zef Wells. I have been slandered and slurred with false accusations, wild conclusions and cruel assumptions. Sadly, the source of this attack is John Tuttle of the Last Hope Baptist Church, who jumped to odious conjectures and leaped to libelous words based upon one troubled individual's confusion. I am a gay man and I did attend one Wiccan service—clothed. In no way does either of these affect my performance as a classroom teacher. I maintain the highest standard of professionalism with my students. Now I will truthfully answer all questions."

Two hundred questions followed, all of which I addressed honestly. I answered questions until the assembled reporters could think of nothing else to ask. Fortunately, no one asked my opinion of deep anal penetration. Either they didn't think about asking it, or the subject was too hot for the news.

Aeslin and I were married in a Wiccan handfasting service two years after we met. Baxter gave me away, and Sal gave Aeslin to me. As the high priest tied the third cord around our wrists, binding us to each other, Al and Julio, the latter now safely eighteen and Al's lover, showered us with flowers and sprinkled us with white wine.

Our handfasting even made the society page of the *Northwest Bugle*. The article made no mention of a fizzled scandal that had rocked the Last Hope Baptist Church two years earlier. It only mentioned that I had been head of the English Department at Millard Fillmore High School for the past year and that Aeslin had been selected as a contestant designer for "Project Runway."

LAST CALL AT THE RAVEN

Simon Sheppard

A misty night out on the Interstate.

Derek shook his head slowly, staring at the fog-wreathed bar. It was a low, nondescript building, the neon reading THE RAVEN now dark over the door. No rainbow flag out front, not for this place deep in closet country. The Raven wasn't a "life-style choice," it was a refuge, the sort of joint that, on a typical Saturday night, played host to guys from miles around: some young student types, others married men sneaking around with hard-ons, a stray would-be leatherman or two, even a sprin-kling of diesel dykes, all slugging down drinks while a local drag queen lip-synched to disco.

The light over the door flashed on, blurry fire-red piercing the dark of night. Derek crossed the parking lot, past Fords and Chevys and a few pickup trucks, and walked up to the entrance. He swung open the heavy door. A blast of heat, music and ciga-rette smoke hit the cool outside air. He crossed the threshold, plunging into the smells of stale beer and deferred desire. The crowd was sparse, no one familiar to him. But then, he hadn't been there in a very long while. As he walked down the length of the dimly lit bar, no one so much as looked up. It wasn't till he was all the way at the back of the long, narrow room that he saw him in the murk, leaning back against the wall.

Jono.

For one long minute, Derek couldn't believe his eyes. Then, slowly, as though not wanting to make Jono dematerialize into the smoke-filled air, he walked toward the man he had loved so long, so deeply. Jono's eyes never left his.

"Fuck," he stammered, when they were, at last, only a foot or two apart, "I thought you..."

"Were gone forever?"

"Yeah." Derek's eyes filled with tears.

"Well, I'm not. Gone forever. As you can see."

"As I can see, yeah." And then he didn't know what to say next. There was so much. There was nothing, really.

"I didn't want to leave you, Derek."

Love is pain, Derek thought. *Oh, god, love is pain.* "I know," he said at last.

Jono reached out his hand. A breeze, somehow cool, passed over Derek's body.

And then the two men fell into each other's arms. The music grew more pounding, insistent. Neither of them minded at all.

And then it was if they were back walking through the woods, the evening they'd first met at the Raven, hand in hand, not caring who saw them.

"This is beautiful," Jono had said, and it had been, the pale moonlight filtering liquidly through the leaves.

And that's when the bashers had struck, three of them coming up from behind, though the injuries hadn't been that bad, really: Jono's lip had been split, Derek had needed a few stitches. And going through the attack hadn't scared them, not really. If anything, it brought them closer together. And that night, Jono had held Derek tight until they both drifted off to a peaceful sleep.

The memory faded, and Derek was back at the Raven. For a moment, Jono seemed to fade in and out of focus, then became solid again.

"I almost lost you," Derek said.

Now it was Jono's turn to look as if he might cry. Derek hugged him again, harder this time, holding on as though he might fade away. They kissed. Jono's mouth tasted of earth.

The already dim light in the bar faded further, all except for a spotlight over a makeshift stage in the corner. Derek moved around beside Jono, and they stood there, arms around each other. Even in the dimness, Derek could see that the bar had filled up a bit, some of the newcomers looking familiar, regulars from back in the day.

The music changed: a gay-bar cliché, "I Will Survive." A plump drag queen with enormous fake tits just barely contained by a sequined dress climbed onstage, lip-synching and gesticulating broadly. Derek remembered her name—Polly Andrus—and smiled. Jono's arm tightened around his waist.

Life is sweet, Derek thought. *So sweet.*

After the beating, Derek and Jono had started seeing each other on a regular basis. It wasn't "dating," not really, since except for nights at the Raven, they didn't go out anywhere together, not even to the movies. Maybe it was because they were still cautious, maybe not. But within a couple of months, Jono had moved into Derek's little house out on the edge of town. Derek went out on his rounds for UPS while Jono stayed at home, making stained-glass boxes that he sold on consignment through antique stores in the area. They loved each other, it turned out, very much.

The drag queen ended her number to a not particularly encouraging smattering of applause. "It's smoky in here. Want to go outside?" Jono asked. Derek hesitated, then agreed. On the way out of the bar, a few of the patrons, the familiar-looking ones, nodded. None of them was a close friend; nobody spoke. But Derek noticed that a few of them, now that he was taken, was with Jono, regarded him with looks of undisguised lust.

The moon was pale and full, the air autumnally chilly. The two men left the red glow cast by the bar's neon sign and walked around the side of the building, out to where the parking lot ended and the field began. In the spectral moonlight, Jono looked almost transparent.

As they stood side by side, Jono reached out for Derek's hand.

"Your hand is cold," Derek said.

"What did you expect?"

It hadn't been easy, living together in an area where male cohabitation was often viewed with suspicion; a suspicion that was, in their case, justified. Still, apart from a few hostile glances at the supermarket, they were mostly left to themselves, and their life together relaxed into a comfortable routine. Derek was the one who did the laundry. Jono cooked. Derek was the one who got fucked, usually. The stained glass boxes that Jono made were featured in a magazine article, and his business grew. Derek was glad for him. Side by side. Comfortably together.

Derek looked out across the fields. "I still love you, you know," he said.

"Of course." Jono's voice was low, almost a whisper. "And I still love you."

"Forever."

"Forever, yes."

And then the symptoms had begun. Nothing very definite at first. Jono felt more tired more often. And then things grew more definite, to where the situation could no longer be denied.

"There are new treatments out there," Derek had said. "New treatments coming along all the time."

But Jono still had grown weaker and weaker, thinner and thinner, until his flesh seemed almost transparent, pale as memory. Derek bought him a topaz and sterling silver ring; it had rattled around on his bony finger.

Toward the end, Jono had said, "I'm only afraid I'll have come and gone, but left no trace. Y'know?"

"My love," Derek had said, "as long as I'm here, you'll be here, too."

Arm in arm now, they looked out across the fields. Cars were pulling in and out of the parking lot, their headlights sweeping across the unnaturally dense mist, right to left, left to right, but the two men seemed to cast no shadows.

"Fuck me," Derek said. "One last time."

Jono nodded. The two walked into a little grove of trees at the edge of the parking lot. There was no one else around. Derek lowered his pants and leaned face-forward against an oak. Using nothing but spit, Jono entered him. There was no resistance.

When they were done, they walked out of the trees, out to the fog-wreathed field.

Jono pressed something into Derek's hand.

The day that Jono died, Derek had gone into the spare room he had used as a studio. One by one, he picked up the stained glass boxes, the half-finished ones, the ones that Jono had completed and were awaiting shipment, and threw them against the wall. Shards of glass littered the floor, shining, colorful.

Derek closed his hand tight around the small, hard object.

"Good-bye, my love." Jono's voice was soft, so soft, as if it were coming from far, far away.

"Don't leave me," Derek said, "again. Please."

No use. Jono smiled at Derek, gave him a squeeze, and set off across the field. As he walked toward the unseen horizon, his form wavered, then dematerialized into nothing, and he was gone.

Derek opened his hand. There in his palm, as anyone would have known it would be, was the silver and topaz ring, illuminated in a swelling golden glow.

Derek, tears in his eyes, turned around. The light was much brighter, redder now. The Raven was on fire, blazing, just the same as it had been years ago, the night it had been torched, the night he had been trapped inside. The night that Derek had died.

He knew that now, after this, he would be with Jono again soon. At least he hoped so. It had to be. Had to.

He walked slowly toward the burning bar, all sparks and smoke, feeling the waves of heat. His body began to smolder. The Raven collapsed inward, like an unreliable memory.

A passing motorist on the Interstate thought for a moment he saw the shadowy shape of a man standing by what was left of what seemed to be a burnt-out ruin. Curious, he slowed down, but there was no one there.

He must have been mistaken.

AWAY IN A MANGER

Tom Mendicino

Whoever wrote that there's no place like home for the holidays never had to travel more than a mile to reach the family hearth by Christmas morning. Year after year, I would make the annual pilgrimage to LaGuardia, watching the meter run while I sat in stalled traffic, shuffling through security and, finally, rushing to the gate, only to be slapped with the announcement of a three-hour delay. I could always count on United Airlines to lose my luggage or overbook the plane or seat me beside a screaming baby. Never again, I swore, after the year I missed my connection at National and had to pay a king's ransom to upgrade to the only available seat on the last flight to Charleston, West Virginia.

So why not put the snappy little BMW 3-Series I kept in the city for summer weekend jaunts to good use? I would drive west through Jersey, dip south through Pennsylvania and Maryland, and be at my mother's house on the far side of West Virginia for dinner.

The first two hundred miles flew by; I was making great time, way ahead of schedule. It was the easiest Christmas sojourn ever, and I was absolutely convinced it was the best idea I'd ever had, right up to the minute the engine died on Interstate 76, my punishment for ignoring the little red light reading MAINTENANCE REQUIRED that had been flashing on the dashboard since sometime after the Fourth of July.

And that's how I found myself in the passenger seat of a tow truck, sitting beside a three-hundred-pound ogre whose right earlobe looked like it had been chewed by a starving pit bull. He was wearing a filthy Steelers jersey, size-sixteen boots and a bright orange hunter's hat that provided some slight reassurance that the bloodstains on the floor had been left by small game and not human prey.

"This goddamn weather is a fucking bitch," he growled as he squinted into the driving rain pounding against the windshield.

The exit ramp off the turnpike announced we were approaching Breezewood, Pennsylvania, the self-proclaimed Town of Motels.

"Guess I'm lucky, breaking down here instead of somewhere else," I said, trying to force a little holiday cheer into the gloom.

"Why's that?" he asked, fumbling in his shirt pocket for a pack of matches.

I figured it wouldn't be wise to ask him not to smoke.

"Not much chance anyone is going to tell me there's no room in the inn in the Town of Motels," I said.

He gave me a blank look, no wattage in his eyes, as if he'd never heard the tale of the birth of the Christ Child.

"You know, like 'Away in a manger, no crib for his bed,'" I said, fumbling, wishing I'd kept my damn mouth shut.

He scowled at my lame attempt at seasonal humor, his eyes

narrowing into threatening slits, wary of being patronized by some suspiciously soft stranger driving a luxury car with a price tag higher than his annual salary.

"Where you from?" he asked in an accusing voice.

"West Virginia. Parkersburg. On the Ohio River. An hour north of Charleston," I answered, not lying about my place of birth.

"How come you have New York plates?" he demanded, determined to make me confess.

"When can someone look at the car?" I asked, trying to change the subject.

"Not until day after tomorrow. No one works on Christmas Day," he said, pulling a flask out of his pocket and, in the spirit of the season, offering me a nip. "So where you want me to drop you off?" I could see he was anxious to start celebrating the traditional redneck Christmas thirty-six-hour drinking marathon. I stared out the window at the phalanx of bright motel signs, each one promising cable TV, premium channels and free continental breakfasts. Quality Court. Quality Inn. Red Roof Inn. Holiday Inn. Travelodge.

"That one," I said, pointing at the Howard Johnson's Motor Lodge up ahead to the right, seduced by happy memories of clam strips and peppermint stick ice cream, wistfully longing for a roadside America that had vanished thirty years ago.

He snorted when I wished him Merry Christmas as he pulled away, dragging my fickle vehicle behind him. The damp, vaguely chemical smell of the motel registration office quickly doused the flickering flame of HoJo nostalgia. The Bengali matron at the front desk was polite yet insistent, somehow managing to seem deferential as she rushed me through check-in. Her sari was the traditional orange of a Howard Johnson's rooftop, but there was no sign of Simple Simon and the Pieman and no dining room or counter. She pointed me to a pair of vending machines when I asked where I could get something to eat. The selection on the Christmas menu was barbecue chips, Butterfingers and Diet Dr. Pepper.

"You don't have a restaurant?" I asked. I felt cheated, scammed, the victim of an unconscionable fraud. This was supposed to be Howard Johnson's! Where were the frankfurters grilled in butter, the macaroni and cheese?

"Restaurant over there. One-half mile," she said, pointing toward the front window and a soaring neon sign, high enough to be seen from the turnpike ridge, announcing that KAY'S KOZY KORNER was the place in town to EAT.

The rain was still coming down hard as I trudged to my room, but the temperature was dropping rapidly. Winter was arriving just ahead of Santa Claus, and I cursed myself for having left my gloves and hat in the car.

It was almost seven o'clock when I called my mother to break the news that I wouldn't be arriving for at least another day and a half. I complained about the shabby state of the hospitality industry, hoping for a little sympathy and maybe leniency for the unpardonable sin of having ruined her Christmas. It was obvious from the tone of her voice she wasn't buying my story and suspected I was actually still in the 10022 zip code and on my way to some glamorous holiday party with my snooty New York friends.

"I'll be there as soon as I can," I promised, unable to convince her that, under the current circumstances at least, there was no place in the world I wanted to be more than sitting down at her table for country ham and ninety-proof eggnog.

"It won't be the same," she said, hanging up to pull her pumpkin pie from the oven.

I was too wired to sleep so I showered and changed into dry

clothes before venturing out on a scavenger hunt for something edible. The rain had changed to a driving snow that had already blanketed the streets and rooftops. The winter storm had transformed the Town of Motels into a department-store window Enchanted Village. It was easy to believe the inflatable Santas and Frostys and Rudolphs were animated by magic when their power cords were buried in snowdrifts. I took a short detour, making a pilgrimage to the illuminated crèche on the lawn of the First Lutheran Church. The town was perfectly still, the only sound the crunch of fresh snow under my feet. I shoved my freezing hands in my pockets and, through swirling gusts of snowflakes, headed toward the EAT sign, quietly singing "Away in a Manger."

The door flew open as I approached, and only my quick reflexes kept me from suffering a broken nose. The tow truck ogre stumbled out of the restaurant, fumbling with his keys, staring at me wild eyed, no glint of recognition on his face. I slipped past him, pitying anyone he encountered on the icy roads tonight, and stepped into a thick fog of cigarette smoke that enveloped me like a blanket. Christmas cheer was flowing from the beer taps. Holiday revelers, mugs in hand, already six sheets to the wind, were howling along to Springsteen's "Santa Claus Is Coming to Town" on the jukebox. It was a rough-looking crowd, weathered by hard work and hard drinking. The girls wore Santa caps and NFL gear, and there was nothing jolly about the men's distended, swollen bellies. A fight broke out at the pool table, and a tray of bottles and glasses shattered on the floor before a fierce-looking dyke in a snowflake sweatshirt could hustle the pugilists out the door.

"Merry Christmas," the boy behind the bar hollered. "What are you drinking?"

"Rye and a beer. Can I get a menu?" I shouted over the scalps of the drinkers hunkered down at the bar, arguing over the best way to eliminate the Muslim threat to their godly American way of life.

"You got a choice. Popcorn or pretzels," he laughed, pointing at the baskets of bar snacks. "The cook called out sick. It's on me," he said, refusing my money as he handed me a shot of Crown Royal and a frosted mug of Bud Lite.

He bounced along the bar, cheerfully pouring booze, taking bills and handing back the change. He knew all the customers by name and smiled through the abuse that was heaped upon him when one of the regulars had to wait longer than twenty seconds for a drink. I was tired and hungry, and the whisky went straight to my head. I set down my empty mug, ready to call it an early night, when another round appeared on the bar. I waved my palm and shook my head, but he insisted I accept the drinks. I figured I should at least tip the kid for his generosity. He frowned and wagged his finger.

"Your money's no good here tonight. Can't accept it," he said, turning away to appease the loudmouth drunk who was cursing him for neglecting his empty glass.

The motel was within stumbling distance, even in a blizzard, and I deserved to get a little buzz going after the shitty day I'd had. I tipped the shot glass to my lips and let the whisky burn my throat. The bartender looked like a college kid, barely of legal drinking age, tall, square jawed, with bright green eyes and a mop of floppy hair. He had the type of sharp features that would grow into a rugged masculinity as the soft layer of baby fat around his jaw and chin melted away with age. His voice, even when shouting, had an eager-to-please pitch that was slightly feminine, but his imposing size, six feet two or three, with broad shoulders, kept him from seeming swishy or obviously gay. He winked when he caught me staring at him—nothing lascivious, just a friendly gesture, his acknowledgment to a stranger who'd wandered into his bar that we were kindred spirits, fellow travelers, despite the obvious twenty- or twenty-five-year difference in our ages.

"What's your name?" he asked as he splashed Absolut and cranberry juice into a glass for a tough-looking babe who'd wedged herself into the crush of drinkers, staking her claim with an elbow planted firmly on the bar.

"What's his name, Jason?" she slurred as she gave me the once-over, her piercing stare made even more unsettling by a lazy left eye.

"Jimmy," I said, using the name I'd been called in my Appalachian boyhood. In New York City, I am known only as James.

"What did he say, Jason?"

"Jimmy."

"Where's he from?" she asked as she fumbled with a crumpled pack of cigarettes. I figured I was safer admitting I was a New Yorker than I had been in the tow truck. And I had an odd, irresistible urge to impress the young bartender.

"La-di-da," she sneered, unimpressed. "You're too old for Jason, Mr. New York. You hear that Jason? He's too old for you."

Something across the room caught her attention and she suddenly lost interest, making a beeline for the jukebox where the dyke in the snowflake sweatshirt and a mullet-coiffed fireplug were looking awfully cozy, singing along to "Merry Christmas, Darling."

"Who's she? Your mother?" I joked, pretending to be miffed by the concerned intervention.

"Who? Wendy?" he laughed. "You got to be kidding. No. *That's* my mother," he said, pointing at Miss Snowflake. "Aunt Wendy's her girlfriend."

I figured I was stone drunk, hearing strange voices and hallucinating that a lesbian militia had invaded this hillbilly backwater on Christmas Eve. I tossed back another shot —my third, or was it fourth?—and cradled a mug of beer while Jason placated the restless natives demanding another round.

"I love New York," he shouted at me as he worked the taps. "I'm gonna move there."

Sure you are, kid, I thought, and snickered. Your senior class probably went to Manhattan for a field trip. Times Square was awesome and *Wicked* changed your life. You're going to find a great apartment like Will's from "Will and Grace" and land a fabulous job as an assistant to a fashion designer or Broadway producer who will recognize you as a genius. In a year, maybe sooner, you'll be rich and famous and have an even richer and more famous boyfriend who will always be faithful and, after New York legalizes gay marriage, you'll have a beautiful wedding and an announcement in the Styles section of the Sunday *Times*. *Christ almighty*, I thought, shocked by my cruel cynicism. When did little Jimmy Hoffman of Parkersburg, West Virginia, become such a misanthrope?

"Right after I graduate," he declared.

"You know New York is pretty expensive. Maybe you should get a job first," I replied, as gently as possible in a loud, obnoxious barroom. I was feeling paternal and sentimental, remembering the little hick from Parkersburg who spent his entire four years at UVA imagining his wonderful life in the bright lights of the magnificent island he had only seen on television and in the movies.

"Oh, I have a job. I interned in a recording studio last summer, and they offered me an apprentice engineer position. I start in June."

I couldn't picture this big country boy, handsome but unpolished, his vowels thickened by a mountain drawl, surviving the city. I was probably confused, hearing only bits and pieces of the conversation, distracted by the noise. Did he say he'd been an intern? Where? Doing what? I'd already forgotten. I was moving beyond a pleasant buzz, well on my way to becoming staggeringly drunk. Time to cut myself off, find my way back to the motel.

"Cheers," he said, pouring two more Crown Royals and proposing a toast. "Nice to meet you, Jimmy. Merry Christmas and Happy New Year."

He swallowed his shot and winked again. His cheerful boyish smile made it impossible for the gesture to look as dirty and suggestive as he intended.

"Don't you be disappearing on me. Mom says I have to close the bar tonight."

I stood by the bed, trying to steady myself, rocking on the balls of my feet.

"Okay, okay, I'm coming," I croaked, hoping to silence the persistent pounding that had roused me from blissful oblivion.

I opened the door and threw my forearm across my face, shielding my bloodshot eyes from the blinding sunlight reflected off the fresh, clean snowdrifts. I was greeted with a "Merry Christmas!" and an awkward peck on the cheek as the boy swept by me, a large bottle of water in one hand and a paper cup of steaming coffee in the other.

"I figured you'd need these. And I wanted to make sure you were awake. You look like you could sleep through the day. Here, drink this first," he said, handing me the water.

I chugged the entire bottle without taking a breath. My dehydrated body could have absorbed three of the five Great Lakes.

"How's your head?"

Not bad actually, considering the amount of alcohol I'd consumed the night before.

"You almost bit off my fingers when I forced you to swallow those aspirin last night."

"You know too much about hangovers for a kid," I protested, my raspy voice cracking and breaking like a pubescent boy's. Christ, was I smoking last night too?

"My mother owns a bar. Remember?"

I did, vaguely. It was coming back into focus. The noise. The whisky and beer. Someone pulling a pistol and waving it at a girlfriend. Pissing on my shoes at the urinal. Something about Boston and the Berklee College of Music. "Rudolph the Red-Nosed Reindeer"...me standing on the bar singing "Rudolph the Red-Nosed Reindeer." Falling on my ass on the ice. A pair of dykes laughing and swearing as they dragged me from the car and threw me on the bed. This boy, Jason, yanking off my pants and pulling the blanket up to my chin, wishing me sweet dreams as he closed the door behind him.

"I gotta get back to church for eleven o'clock Mass. I'll pick you up around twelve-thirty. You didn't forget, did you?"

I must have looked perplexed.

"You're coming to my mom's for Christmas dinner. It'll be fun."

He grabbed my unshaven cheeks and kissed my stale, sour mouth.

"I've been wanting to do that since the first minute I saw you," he said, blushing as he turned to leave, leaving me stunned, my knobby knees shaking and my boner stirring in the baggy crotch of my boxers.

According to Jason, three-and-half-million cars exit the turnpike through Breezewood every year, but not a single soul actually lives there. We sped past the last stoplight and plunged into the wilderness, my still bloodshot eyes protected from the snow glare by a pair of borrowed sunglasses.

"You're not kidnapping me, are you? I don't want to end up

like *Texas Chainsaw Massacre,*" I chuckled, joking of course, but slightly apprehensive about leaving the last evidence of civilization, such as it was, miles behind.

"Don't worry. You're in Pennsylvania. The serial killers are much cuter up here."

He reached over, squeezed my knee and growled, doing a damn good imitation of a buzz saw.

"Do you have a boyfriend?" he asked.

"No, I don't have a boyfriend."

"Nice."

"Do you know how old I am?"

"Old enough to have a lot of gray hair."

Well, only since last summer, when I stopped coloring it after the famous cable news anchor I was blowing in the Meat Rack on the Island commented that my hair was the same shade of purple as the bruise on his elbow.

"What makes you so sure I'm gay?" I challenged him, changing the subject.

"Um...could it have been...maybe...let me think...the P-town sweatshirt you were wearing last night?"

"What do you know about P-town?" I asked, sounding awfully petulant and irritated for a man who was about to turn only forty-four.

"I told you last night. I live in Boston."

Yes, yes he did. Berklee College of Music—he's a dual major, studying music production and engineering, because he needs to make a living, and performance, because guitar is his passion, the most important thing in his life. He's going to support himself working in the studio and play at every open mike in every coffeehouse and dive bar in Manhattan and Brooklyn, Queens even, until he gets his big break. He made me ashamed about sneering at his dreams, this kid who was so much better prepared to take on New York than a certain naïve young alumnus of Charlottesville who'd arrived in Gotham with a degree in English and great ambitions, only to discover that the hiring editors at Scribner's and Knopf weren't interested in anything on his resume except the score on his typing test.

"I'm glad you don't have a boyfriend," he said, his goofy grin illuminating his face. "I like older guys."

I smiled and shook my head no, discouraging him, then turned and stared at the pristine fields outside the window, thinking about someone I hadn't seen for many years, a ghost from the long-ago past when I liked older guys too.

Wendy was sprawled on the living room floor, her head and shoulders wedged between the wall and the Christmas tree.

"Flip the switch," she shouted, apparently not passed out, then bounced up on her feet, as the locomotive of a classic Lionel Pennsylvania Flyer O-Gauge model train successfully relaunched after derailing off the platform.

"It never runs off the track where it's easy to reach," she sighed, resigned to the misfortunes of model railroading. The display under the tree was damn impressive: two freight trains and a passenger line running on multiple level tracks through a scale model of the Town of Motels.

"Aunt Wendy, you remember my friend Jimmy from last night?" She took a deep breath and drew herself up to full height, an impressive five two at best. She seemed a bit softer than last night, in her fuzzy white holiday vest with red yarn candy canes embroidered on the panels, but her voice was as intimidating as it had been in the bar.

"He's still too old for you, Jason. But I'm not your mother," she said, her lazy eye drifting toward the train platform.

"Leave him alone," the lady of the house barked, setting a

tray with an orange cheese ball and Ritz crackers on the coffee table.

My heart jumped in my chest, unfairly convicted and sentenced for a crime I hadn't committed.

"Look," I blurted, "I'm not planning on robbing any cradles."

Jason's mother cocked an eyebrow and grumbled in a low, threatening voice.

"What's the matter? Our Jason isn't good enough for you?"

"Ma," he pleaded. "She's just messing with you, Jimmy. Ma, leave him alone. It's Christmas."

She giggled apologetically, a tough woman turning unexpectedly shy and girlish as she capitulated to her child.

"Jason, why don't you tell your friend to have a seat."

"His name's Jimmy, Mama."

She extended her hand for a formal introduction.

"Kay Previc. Very nice to meet you. Again."

She cut a wedge of cheese and offered it to me on a cracker. Aunt Wendy poured out four glasses of sparkling cider and proposed a toast.

"I don't keep alcohol in the house," Kay announced. "We see enough of that at the bar. No need to bring it into our home."

I felt defensive, suspecting she'd made a wrong assumption about my relationship with alcohol based on my completely out-of-character behavior the prior night.

"I'm not a big drinker anyway," I asserted.

"There's nothing wrong with being a drinker. That's how I put food on the table and gas in the tank."

I simply nodded, it being obvious that even my most conciliatory attempts at polite conversation would be challenged. Aunt Wendy tossed back her cider, twitchy and nervous, resigned to the imposition of Prohibition in the household.

"It's very nice you could join us today, Jimmy," Kay declared after a long, awkward silence.

"Thank you for having me," I mumbled, swallowing a mouthful of dry, salty cheddar.

The strain of trying to entertain me was exhausting. Kay quickly abandoned any pretense of playing hostess and sank into an easy chair in front of the television, falling dead asleep during the second half of a Pistons/Mavericks holiday showdown. Jason suggested we go for a walk, obviously wanting to take advantage of this opportunity to spend a few a moments alone. He gave me a wool cap and a pair of gloves and looped a scarf around my neck, pulling it gently, a solicitous, maternal touch. The rubber boots he handed me fit well enough over my shoes, a little large maybe, but manageable.

The sun had lost its midday brilliance and the afternoon had turned a soft, pale gray. Another storm was massing above the mountain range and the wind was rising, rustling through the bare tree branches.

"I think it's going to snow again," I said, worried about being stranded in this desolate outpost where snowplows seldom ventured, certainly never on Christmas Day.

"It will be real pretty when it does. Wait and see," he said, beckoning me to follow him down a steep, ice-crusted lane that descended through a thicket of soaring birch trees.

"Are you okay?" he asked, turning and reaching for my hand.

"Sure," I said, my uncertain footing betraying my false bravado.

A dog barked in the distance and some unseen creature bolted through the dense undergrowth. Jason was standing at the bottom of the hill, holding a broken branch like a staff. He lifted it above his head and slammed it into the ground, puncturing the sheath of ice beneath his feet. The water gurgled as it raced below the frozen surface.

"Don't worry," he laughed. "It's only a creek. No danger of drowning."

Still, the crunchy crush of yielding ice wasn't reassuring. I liked my toes too much to lose them to frostbite.

"We're standing on the Susquehanna watershed. When I was a little kid I dreamed about building a raft and taking it all the way to the ocean."

"Like *Huckleberry Finn.*"

"Yeah," he laughed. "Except I've never read that book, but I think I saw the movie."

He took a lumbering step toward me, threw open his arms, and wrapped me in a tight bear hug. The dull white sun was barely visible behind a shroud of thin, hazy clouds.

"My dad shot himself down here when I was eight," he confided. "On the first day of school after Christmas. The ambulance was taking him away when the bus dropped me off. I burnt down the barn that summer. My mother always says it was an accident. But I started the fire on purpose."

He turned away, not wanting to see the expression on my face, and started back up the lane. He stopped when he reached the crest of the hill, waiting for me, and as I stood next to him, he turned to survey the horizon, range after range of the ancient Alleghenies still visible in the dying light, carpeted with hibernating hardwoods waiting, as ever, to blossom again in the spring. Snow was blowing in from the north and the sun finally expired in a last gasp of bright violet streaks that trailed beyond the farthest visible mountain ridge. I thought for a moment he was crying but realized it was only snowflakes melting on his broad cheeks.

"It is pretty, isn't it?" he asked, his expectant face looking impossibly vulnerable. "I wanted to tell you about what I did so you would know from the beginning, just in case you might think you could like me."

The meal was simple. A turkey breast with sausage stuffing, candied yams, jellied cranberry. Aunt Wendy didn't seem to have much of an appetite except for the red velvet cake we had for dessert; she excused herself, pleading fatigue, while the three of us cleared the table.

"Her diabetes is out of control," Kay fretted. "She refuses to take care of herself. Shoots up with insulin, then helps herself to a piece of lemon meringue pie."

I could see she was preparing to embark on her second widowhood, having given up on Wendy as a lost cause. I suspected the younger woman with the mullet was the insurance policy she'd taken out against a lonely future.

"You boys leave me to finish up in here. Go enjoy the rest of Christmas," she insisted, taking a scouring pad to the roasting pan.

"What's your favorite Christmas song?" Jason asked as we settled on the sofa, the only light the soft glow of the tree.

"Not 'Rudolph,'" I swore, cringing at the memory of last night.

"Good."

"'The Hallelujah Chorus.'"

He looked exasperated, shaking his head.

"That's Easter! Everyone thinks it's Christmas music, but it's an Easter chorus! I had to play it as the recessional at the eight-thirty and eleven o'clock Masses today. It was ridiculous!"

"Then why did you do it?"

"Because the Catholics pay me twenty-five bucks a service. That's fifty bucks. And the priest gave me an extra twenty-dollar tip. That's good money."

"But you like Handel?"

"I love Handel."

He jumped up and bolted from the room, returning with a guitar and sheet music.

"You're lucky. I've got a score, but it's arranged for a guitar quartet. A bunch of us whore ourselves out, doing crap like Sunday brunches at the Ritz. We don't even have to practice since no one really listens. They'd rather eat waffles and get shit-faced on mimosas. Hang on. It's gonna take me a minute to work this out."

He screwed his face into a pantomime of concentration as he studied the notes on the page, muttering instructions to himself. He ran his long, tapered fingers through his thick hair and announced he'd figured out how to play this solo. No promises, he said, but he was sure he could do a pretty decent job.

"Close your eyes and think of a full orchestra," he said, his voice brimming with quiet confidence. He tweaked the tuners and, finally satisfied, began to play.

The intensity of his focus, the power of his concentration, was astonishing and unexpected. Only a moment ago he'd been a boy, awkward and eager to impress. His poise and command of his instrument was intimidating. His mastery of the neck was total and complete as his fingers coaxed a chorus of voices from the six strings.

"So? What do you think?" he asked, as the final note faded, seeking a sign of approval.

The question left me mystified and feeling inadequate since any words of praise would seem facile, patronizing.

"But can you play 'Blue Christmas'?" I asked, retreating to the comfort zone where sarcasm is a brittle shield and a wry retort the best defense.

He smiled and strummed a few open chords as he sang the

familiar lyrics. He didn't try any humorous attempts at Elvis-like vocal pyrotechnics, no campy gulps and throbs. His simple, sincere voice, direct and unaffected, was steeped in the all-too-familiar soul-crushing loneliness of a boy who feared he'd never be loved.

He played until long after midnight and, when it was finally time for bed, he sprawled on the sofa beside me, tucked into the long crevice of my body, gripping my hand through the night. I slept in fits, never yielding to an aching arm or twisted knee, not wanting to disturb him, begrudging the face of my watch as the hours crawled toward the inevitable daybreak. In the not-too-distant future, this Christmas would become the stuff of legend, enhanced with each recitation for my jaded New York audience, a made-for-television holiday movie about two mismatched strangers, fate throwing them together for a single night and a memory that would last a lifetime.

Two days (and a seven-hundred-dollar Visa charge to a certain Breezewood mechanic) later, I finally arrived in West Virginia to celebrate the birth of Our Lord with my mother and the carcass of a country ham. I resisted the temptation to call Pennsylvania under the pretense of thanking the Prevics for their hospitality, but my mind kept wandering back to the lumpy sofa in a remote farmhouse where a gentle, needy boy clung to me through the night. I checked my emails before bed and found a short note from Jason, wishing me a Happy New Year and saying he hoped he could call me when he arrived in New York next summer. Three photos were attached: one was of his sweet, boyish face, grinning at the digital camera he held an arm's length away; the second was of his thick, erect cock; and the third was an awkward shot, one-handed, of his bare ass.

I really, really like you, he signed off.

I cut my West Virginia visit short, pleading an emergency

editorial conference with a newly signed author who was about to announce his presidential ambitions. Aunt Wendy was the first to spot me when I walked through the door of the Kozy Korner. She whispered something to Kay, who tried to suppress a cautious smile as I approached her son's broad back. *There's going to be a lot of heartache before this is all over,* I thought as I tapped him on the shoulder, remembering a different man's sad, resigned face, his eyes wet with tears as I announced I needed to be around people my own age, too much of a coward to admit I was already involved with another editorial assistant in my office whose ass didn't sag and who didn't need forty minutes to get an erection.

Jason arrived in June, taking me up on my offer of a crash pad until he saved enough for a deposit on a hovel in Willamsburg or Jersey City. He stayed for seven years, until the vast differences in our ages led to the inevitable fissures and tension that threatened to harden into intractable anger and resentment, and I knew it was time to set him free. He never strays too far, though, always needing a safe place to retreat when his still-young heart suffers yet another disappointment. And every year, on Christmas Eve, he throws his bag in the trunk and tucks his guitar in the backseat and we head west through New Jersey, and dip south through Pennsylvania, where we spend the night together in a farmhouse outside the Town of Motels before I push on for West Virginia in the morning.

PORCU MEU

Derrick Della Giorgia

When I smoke a cigarette on my balcony in via Collazia, I am precisely 1.9 kilometers away from the Coliseum, 3.6 kilometers south of the Trevi Fountain and 6.2 kilometers outside of the Vatican. I am surrounded by the historical center of Rome. I am immersed in what people travel the world to see. Notwithstanding, in no way is that cigarette comparable to the one I smoke in the garden of my family house in Muro Leccese. And the elation that the five thousand inhabitants of the village cause in my globe-trotter's head is even more exceptional during the village festival, a real localized holiday: *Porcu Meu.*

Porcu Meu, the shameless dialectal translation of My Pork, takes place every year in October, usually the second or third weekend of the month. In the south, almost every village has its special holiday dedicated to the most pagan celebration of community life; mine, so far south in the heel of the boot that it is closer to North Africa than to the rest of Europe, had chosen pigs to reunite once a year five thousand hearts under a few electric bulbs, the moonlight and the loud folkloric music emanating from speakers tied to people's balconies in the main square. At the age of twenty-seven, I can count on one hand the times I have missed *Porcu Meu*. Certainly, I was not going to miss it this year...

My crush on the village butcher's son has haunted me since August, when for the first time in my life I ventured into the butcher shop and bought steaks for dinner. Separated as we were by the chilled flesh between us, our first conversation infected my brain with the virulence of a computer bug. His husky words, neatly separated by the banging of his knife on the wooden counter, planted into my head the unquenchable desire to have sex with the young man wearing a blood-spattered white vest.

My summer vacation passed quickly as my family increased, without realizing why, its intake of beef, sausage and other meats dispensed in the busy shop on via Corsica. Despite inflating my levels of cholesterol and torturing myself at night trying to realize from my fantasies what my body sought from the young butcher's hands and lips, I was not scoring much. Jacopo—his father had spoken his name once—was as cordial with me as he was reserved, an inflammatory combination that followed me when I returned by train to Rome at the beginning of September.

"When are you coming back, now?" asked my mum, her voice already nostalgic when she called my Rome apartment, as usual, the day after I left Muro Leccese.

"*Porcu Meu,* I can't wait!" I said, guilty because the excitement in my response was uniquely dictated by my hunger for seeing Jacopo and had nothing to do with my mum's love.

On my balcony, behind the Coliseum and south of the Vatican, my only thoughts were dedicated to him, and as summer faded into the mild chill that anticipates the winter holidays, I completely fell in love with the memory of Jacopo, fantasizing day after day about his short corvine hair, longer on the top and almost shaved on the sides; about his provocative lips; about the tribal tattoo that climbed from his left elbow and up his muscled arm all the way to his solid deltoid. I calculated that it had taken me about five hundred euros worth of meat to glimpse all of that tattoo: the lower part he revealed to me when in the heat of a busy moment he pulled the sleeves of his white coat up and the upper part when he was wearing a tank top the only time I was in the shop as he was changing to leave.

Lithe, tall, without a trace of a beard despite his twenty-three years, taciturn, with the look of a bored naughty angel, Jacopo was the newest obsession of my life; my friends were getting tired of hearing about him. But Muro Leccese was a small village, and I couldn't simply ask him out to see if he was interested in getting to know me. Deciphering his inclinations from his behavior wasn't an option either; he was too cryptic to be interpreted. We had no friends in common; I had no time to create a bridge between us during the hardly twenty days I had spent in August away from my beloved computers. Only *Porcu Meu* could offer the opportunity. For the festival, the eight butchers of the village prepared tons of pork and sold it all night long to happy people relaxed by red wine and familiar music. Yes, *Porcu Meu* could provide me with a chance to explore his feelings for me: a long night in proximity to him, bathed by the perfumed boiled pork that sprayed warm smoke in the streets and above the houses around the square.

Exactly a month and a half after my reflections on how to conquer my prey, punctual as a burp after a Coke, music started filling the streets of Muro Leccese at 8:00 P.M., and the people of the village knew that that succulent pork only needed lemon and black pepper to be savored. Families showed up first, especially if the kids were very young, then elders followed, and finally everyone else made his appearance, and the consumption of wine and the volume of music hit the roof. I accompanied my father when he bought a sufficient amount of pork for our dinner, and I quickly ate at the house—my family preferred to transport the party home instead of eating in the street—before returning to the open air. Even at 11:00 P.M. my beautiful butcher boy was besieged by hungry hundreds eager for meat. He kept bouncing back and forth like the shuttle of a loom from the garage where the meat was cooked to his stand on the sidewalk, where he handed juicy cuts of pig to customers. I leaned against the wall a few feet away and sipped wine from a white plastic cup, wondering how at last to approach him—even to seduce him—without creating a scandal.

It was then, between a first cigarette and a second cup of wine, that I discovered I wasn't the only fan of the sexy butcher. A fifteen-year-old girl kept jumping up and down when she finally was in front of him, urging her friend to take a picture of him when he wasn't looking. Jacopo spotted his young female admirer and ventured a subtle, hormone-raising smile. The night's wine must have loosened up his prudish reticence. His come-on to her, however, was a green flag for my indecisive state of mind: I checked my outfit, making sure my white shirt was unbuttoned to the point where the butcher boy could get a nice view of my smooth, fit chest—and with some extra luck my pierced right nipple—and I moved toward him with the intention of asking him whether he would like to have a cup of wine with me when he was done.

There were only two rows of people between us; I circled

the counter and stopped behind the register, the only patch where people were not standing. But before I was able to enact the script I had carefully written in my mind during the weeks before my return to the village for this fateful night, he turned to me and twisted everything.

"Hi, there. I am dying for a cigarette. I'm done in five, would you offer me one?" he asked shamelessly, to my happy surprise.

"Sure," I managed to reply. "I'm going to get another cup of wine, catch me over there." The alcohol I had imbibed rendered me uninhibited enough to answer.

"Got it." He winked and went back to serving the crowds.

Two sips of my new cup of wine later, I was standing in front of him, commenting on the joyful night and the success of the festival, while quietly admiring his body, for the first time not veiled by a butcher's smock.

"I'll get you another one of those and we can walk to the park. I really need to sit down and smoke a cigarette. What do you say?" He walked past me and extracted his wallet from the back pocket of his jeans, awarding me with the sweet vision of his tight ass. I also noticed for the first time his right ear was pierced and that he had changed his haircut since the summer.

"Sounds awesome. I need to sit too. I'm kind of buzzed," I lied, hoping my claim of inebriation might justify whatever crazy gesture my desire for him would push me to commit. As it was, I was barely able to keep my hands from searching his baggy clothes for the muscles underneath. I still couldn't believe that I was going to get him—and I hadn't even had to ply my seductive wiles. *He has already offered himself*, I exulted. I wanted to fast forward to where we kissed and touched each other in the dark of the *Porcu Meu*.

"Let's go!" he commanded, clutching three cups of wine. He

fended off the crowds with veteran mastery, guiding us through streets that became gradually more quiet to the most tranquil and isolated bench in the park, halfway between my house and the festivities.

"Ahh... I can't believe I can finally rest my ass!" He sprawled on the bench and leaned back, gulping down almost half of the first cup of wine. "Can I have that cigarette now?"

"Here is your deserved cigarette..." No matter how much wine he might have had, I was struck by how his summer shyness had vanished, how his ability to interact with me had gone from limited to limitless.

"Much better." He moaned after the first drag. I was standing in front of him, in doubt about how to act. Something told me that his new imperiousness could only be a sign of his heterosexuality. "Sit!" he commanded: imperious, even pompous, but hot, sexy, mouthwatering, crotch inflating. What did I have to lose?

The chill of the night was more bitter in the park, and the white of the moon looked colder and farther away than it had in the music-wrapped festival square half an hour earlier. Jacopo didn't say anything for a while, and I accepted the silence as a test of how far we might really go, of how much more of each other we were willing to discover.

"So..." I turned to him, but before I could question his intentions, he slowly moved his head toward mine, five, four, three inches away, his square head obstructing the moon, and I smelt his skin, pungent like early morning summer sex. My heart skipped a beat and my chest tightened. I tasted the red wine and the tobacco on his lips as he pressed them against mine. I trapped his upper lip into mine and dove in for more...but he rapidly withdrew and left me midair, with my mouth parted and my eyes closed.

"I am so sorry…I am not gay…" He stood and started gesticulating, as if preparing to contain the eruption of rage surging within me.

"What the fuck is your problem?" I was so confused that I didn't really know what was going through my mind; probably a mix of desire and excitement and rage and embarrassment.

"I can explain, wait!" He picked up his cell phone and scrolled through numbers, still flailing one arm.

"Yes! Explain!" No, I was not embarrassed, I was pissed. What was the asshole trying to prove?

"I am not gay, but my brother is…" he stammered.

"Are you insane? Did you cook your brain with the pork? Let me see if I understand what just happened. Just because I am gay and your brother is too, he and I were going to hook up? I have never seen him!"

"Fabrizio, calm down. I have a twin brother. And you *do* know him. His name is Jacopo. I am *Daniele*." He waited for a reaction.

I was struck speechless. I stared at him, hoping he would continue.

"He likes you, from the shop. He spends hours talking about you. He thinks you're sexy. He asked around to learn your name. But he's shy. No matter how many times I told him to talk to you, he was afraid to. He is home sick tonight. When I saw you, I recognized you, and I knew you thought I was him…so...do you understand now?"

"You are still an asshole. Maybe less of an asshole than before, but still an asshole…did you have to kiss me?"

"I'm not good with words. But I had to know if you were really attracted to him, and if I had rebuffed you, I would have pushed you away from *him*, and I would have never forgiven myself."

The screen of his phone lit the distance between us. I snatched it from him and heard a voice answer, a voice subtly different from the one I had just been speaking with, a voice I heard in my heart.

"Happy *Porcu Meu!* Your brother just kissed me...and I thought I was kissing you!"

I spend much more time back in the village of my birth now, many kilometers from the Coliseum and the Trevi Fountain and the Vatican, and with my darling Jacopo I have all the meat I want to eat.

YOU'RE A DOG

Edward Moreno

The Big Fella

They say a man's heart is as big as his fist. I have no reason to dispute that, but in Ben's case it begs the question. His heart must be the size of a bucket; I accept that.

I met him on the almost-leafy banks of the Yarra, on that almost-green promenade in Melbourne's liquid heart. There's something about Melbourne I've never liked—something hard. I feel most times like I've been bent by the wind, hung out to dry by the drought, leveled by the tough, flat surface of the city. Every leaf on every tree is edged in brown, every footpath a display of dust. It's not pretty, but it's home.

I've never been one for pretty anyway.

"You're a dog," he said—the first thing he said to me. "You're an ugly motherfucker."

He came right up to me—his enormous feet practically trod on mine—and his eyes widened. He brought his face close, getting an eyeful, then pulled back to look me up and down, head to toe, and cracked a smile.

"I can't even stand to look at you," he said and turned away, looked up the river to Prince's Bridge, then twisted his torso back toward me and said it again. *You're a dog.*

I didn't take it badly. I've been broken, bent and trod on over the years—my face and body are crisscrossed with scars, I'm not pretty—but I was taken aback. I hadn't met anyone this forward in years. I couldn't help but stare after catching sight of him sprawled across the bluestone pillars on the water's edge—his long legs stretched out across the promenade, the river at his back—and the next thing I knew he was in front of me, telling me what a dog I was and asking for my number.

His hair was shaggy, a lion's mane, but his twentysomething face was keen edged, fine and dark. Whenever he spoke, he'd open his eyes wide and run them over the whole of my face, my body, nodding to confirm the truth of whatever he'd just said—but when he talked about what a dog I was he'd shake that shaggy head and turn away, look up or down the river and then look back at me, dark eyes ablaze. We exchanged the basics as he moved in and out of my space—coming in close, inspecting me, stepping back.

Buskers spruiked their shows in his shadow on the promenade, families with prams rolled past; the brown leaves of the plane trees crackled in the dry wind, and Ben circled me like a boxer in the ring.

He had my attention. He sized me up, He stepped back and balled his bucket-sized hands into fists. He landed two quick jabs on my chest. He came in close again, looking down at our toes, drawing my eyes down, his enormous toes and my trembling toes almost touching. He said, "Man, I'd love to go toe-to-toe with you."

He gave me an eyes-wide nod and then turned on his heel,

looming as he sauntered away on his chunky legs; shaggy headed, yes, but clean and crisp in his preppy jumper and his A&F shorts, walking light in his loafers, a pretty but gigantic young man who'd just called me a dog.

At home five minutes later, I mentioned nothing to Ivan, just double-checked my face in the mirror, to make sure I wasn't that much of a dog. I couldn't decide either way—I'd had a bottle broken in my face in a bar fight, and one of the scars from that night rambles right across my uneven nose. I inspected it and wondered about the meaning of toe-to-toe. In the bed or in the ring? It didn't matter. I smiled at my image before—absently, distractedly—joining Ivan on the couch.

We fumbled around in front of the TV, and I squeezed a few big-hearted cuddles out of my Ivan, and he laid a strip of kisses across my chest, while the TV couples and comedy families squabbled and one-lined each other. We fell asleep at some point, intertwined and sweating wherever our skin touched, behind my knees and on my chest where his head rested. I woke up a little later, untwined myself and went for a swim.

In the Pool

When I'm in the pool everything liquefies, myself included. On solid ground I feel fairly square with the boundaries between myself and other objects in the world, but in the pool those straight lines fall away and everything collapses and I whirl through the water, digging the sound it makes as it percolates through my head. I take pleasure in stretching time and space: I'm infinite when I extend my arm again and again—I'm the universe.

That night I swam for over an hour in my endless bubble state, watching the navy-blue tile floor revolve below me and around me like a marble globe, while outside the sky darkened above the city and the orange clouds moved through me, inside and outside the building. It was good to be in the water then, with everything mixing together, with all the lines blurred, with the tiles and the city undulating past, rolling past without end, and me thinking of the giant boy with his giant hands, his heart the size of a bucket, his wide-eyed gaze.

My body was rubber when I pulled myself out of the water, into the dark.

Ivan was doing push-ups at the foot of the bed when I walked back into the apartment. He finished and looked at me, his chest and face galah-pink from pumping out a set. I smiled. "Have you always been such an ugly fucker, or is this something new?"

I didn't ruffle his feathers—no one could, he was unruffleable. He just laughed. "Don't tell me you're only just working that out."

There's something that separates Ivan and me, and it's not just the quiet space between us, or the length of the hall, or even where I end and he begins. Sometimes we're so close—I'll be inside him, or he'll be inside me—and I'll be free-falling without a net.

Right Fist

I sat on the sofa in front of the TV with the sound turned down. I looked at my hands: one held the TV remote; the other cupped my balls through my tracksuit pants. Ivan was in bed. Watching porn in semidarkness is like moving through water: time stretches out and nearly slows to a stop; my right fist becomes the universe; lines and boundaries blur when I'm bathing in the blue TV light.

I'm only interested in the beginning—the very beginning—of the encounter: the first flicker of possibility, the first glance, the first moment one man begins to lean his head toward the other's, the unbuttoning of the top button. I shoved my hand into the waistband of my tracksuit, watching the men on the screen as they caught each other's eyes, gave each other a second glance. I rocked my cock in my right fist while the other fist rocked the remote, pausing, replaying in slow motion, pausing, replaying, pausing, replaying; recalling the exact moment earlier in the day when I first caught sight of Ben, with his long legs like tree trunks, his arms like tree branches: that exact moment when one guy first moves toward the other.

In the morning, Ivan woke me with his regular routine. He grinned over the ironing board, nodding toward my right arm, immobilized by my waistband, and asked, "How you going there, champ?"

"I could use a hand," I said.

"Looks like you're doing all right there by yourself."

I watched him from the black hole of the sofa that had swallowed me overnight. The rain that morning was heavy—it darkened the sky, and the apartment and the rest of the world—and since I never liked working in other people's gardens in such rain, I decided to reschedule all my work.

"I could use a hand," I said again, nodding toward my crotch, right hand still thrust down the front of my pants.

"How do I look?" he asked and turned so I could get a look at his arse in his suit pants, then turned again to face me. He looked great, with sexy close-cropped salt-and-pepper hair and his Paul Newman eyes. His chest pressed tight against the light blue fabric of his shirt as he tied his tie.

"You're a bit too sexy, I think."

"That's always going to be a problem. Not much we can do about it."

We both smiled, and Ivan gave my cock and balls a squeeze and me a kiss before he headed out the door.

I lay on the sofa listening to the rain fall before eventually pulling my hand off my cock, and then I set out candles on the altar, crossed my fingers and toes and prayed to the stars and the universe that Big Ben would give me a call, invite me round to his place, fuck me silly and then punch me in the head.

He called as soon as I lit the last candle, and the clouds cleared and the sun broke through.

I'm not sure why I said yes, when my real life proclivities—just like my porno predilections—tend toward the very first movements, toward intention and nothing more.

Pause

I floated up Spencer Street in the rain, uphill, upstream in the downpour, aware of my surroundings, of the lines laid out across the landscape of the city—tracks, footpaths—of the flashing orange lights on the green and yellow trams, of the colossal oversized-egg-carton roof of Southern Cross Station, of the umbrella-wielding mobs. I kept inside my own private rectangle, upright on solid ground, watching the lines intersect and diverge, diverge and intersect. Serpent trams hissed and rattled.

Ben lived at the top of a tower at the bottom of Latrobe Street. I looked at my ugly face in the mirror as I went up in the lift, smiled at the devil in it and at my crooked nose. You'd think I'd recognize the guy I saw, but he was always an interesting stranger with a confused look.

Big Ben answered the door in baggy sweatpants, shirtless, with a serious case of bed head that suited the young, thick, brute. He was about as wide and thick as I was tall, and a good foot and a half taller. We sat on his balcony while he smoked a cigarette that almost disappeared in a hand the size of a dinner plate. It looked like a little redhead matchstick.

The rain had stopped, but his balcony was wet. While he

smoked, I tended his potted plants, a veritable garden—herbs and tomatoes, flowering shrubs, poinsettias and even a couple of frangipani. I couldn't help but do the gardening thing.

The sky had turned purple, the temperature had risen and something was brewing in the sky. I leaned on the air-conditioning unit next to Ben's giant body while he watched me, cigarette between his thumb and forefinger, and wished I could push pause at that exact moment. He breathed out the cigarette smoke, which hung in the air like a cloud far above my head. I watched it circle and storm like the clouds just beyond the balcony rail, then saw the big fella begin to lean his dark scruffy face toward mine.

I'm not sure when it started, this pulling back, this desire to stop everything at just that moment. It's much more beautiful, though—the pending moment. So I looked at his thick lips, breathed in the air (rainfall, frangipani, cigarette smoke, recent sleep, a young man's breath, neck sweat), negotiated his unshaven jawline with my eyes (big as a sisal doormat as it got closer), saw out of the corner of my eye his big hand flick a cigarette over the balcony rail before starting on its way toward my waist or my crotch, saw his lips opening, saw the tip of his thick tongue, breathed his recent sleep scent again and sensed my cock stirring in my jocks. I watched it all and felt it inside me, smelled it, saw him moving in slow motion, his red lips, the red ember of his cigarette tumbling over the side of the balcony.

I think it's safer to stop there and somehow more satisfying. It always has been, in my life. There's no free-fall that way, only solid ground, and it all felt very solid just then, in the big man's grasp, on that balcony in the sky. I paused for one more beat, watched the purple clouds moving behind Ben's shaggy brown mane, and then the storm started. He landed a kiss and we breathed the same air, his mouth tasted like sex, and I felt it inside me and at the tip of my cock, and then the cyclone started.

I swear to god that's exactly what happened. His bucket-sized heart beating against my chest, my own heart filled like a bucket, my cock knocked against his through my jocks and jeans and his tracksuit pants.

Left Fist

And then Ben punched me in the head just like I thought he would, the big giant. I saw a flash of light and my head exploded. I should've known not to climb up into the giant's lair looking for the golden egg when I knew he wanted to go toe-to-toe with me, to tell me what an ugly fucker I was. *Now why'd I have to go and do that?* I thought as my knees buckled.

It was another pause moment, the bright white light, the sound of something popping, and the brief flash of pain before my body collapsed and blood flowed. I thought of Ivan, his big chest under his blue-striped tie, his blue eyes; thought of the time I got hit by a cricket bat at school; thought of my own fear of everything, of my inability to get really close to another man; and then the blood poured more, a lot of it, and I tasted it, and Big Ben caught me in his full-size arms.

Only a few minutes later, I woke up in Ben's bed, inside his arms, my startled head against his slab of a chest, my neck cradled by his tender left hand. He was a gentle nurse, cleaning up my bloody head, my angry eye. *Ouch*. It was only then, looking up at his chunky head as he looked after me, that I started to work out what had happened—he'd saved the hailstone that had clocked me, and he showed it to me before chucking it out the window.

"Won't be needing that," he said, winking at me.

Big Ben had a heart the size of a bucket, and he was filling me up with love. He tended my wound and we had a tender fuck and the big fella pumped me full of big love, while the rain continued to fall.

Outside the city was in chaos, we heard nothing but sirens and alarms. Ben was gazing at me sideways with a curious look on his face.

"And I thought you were a dog before!" he said, giving me the once-over, pausing at the damage. "You're a sexy fucker, and those bruises just help to make you look better. You got some character, you ugly bastard."

I laughed, kept laughing while I dressed, looking at my purple face in the mirror. Ben caught my eye a couple of times and winked.

Sexy," he said.

I was still wobbly, and the world was blurry, so Ben offered to walk me home. Feeling tenderized, I said yes.

Heart

We had to splash through knee-high water part of the way, under cataracts and around broken glass, and at one point the big fella threw me over his shoulder like a rag doll while he waded through waist-high water up Clarendon Street. A kayaker passed us by just then, and we gave each other a wink and a smile, appreciating the other's choice of transportation.

It looked like the drought was over, and I was pleased to see Melbourne this way, liquid, underwater, softer.

We waded through thigh-high water just to get into the lobby of my building. The lift was out, so we climbed seven flights of stairs to my apartment. My balcony garden was destroyed, my terra-cotta pots broken and scattered, soil twirled in an eddy, mixed with a world of brilliant white hailstones and thousands of bright, shredded emerald leaves.

"It's a mess, but it's kind of beautiful, innit?" Ben said, watching the mess swirl in the wind.

He left me with my bucket on the balcony, to salvage my plants.

Ivan found me on the couch later, nursing my throbbing head.

"What the fuck happened to you?" he asked as soon as he came in the door, shoes and socks off, pants rolled up to his knees.

"God gave me a big punch in the head."

"What the fuck?"

"A hailstone the size of your fist clocked me."

He's a doll, my Ivan, and he fell straight onto the couch where he could hold me in his arms and plant a kiss on my damaged head, inspecting it up close.

"You're going to have a serious black eye."

I told him it was killing me and he insisted on the hospital, but I was more obstinate than he was and instead we curled up on the sofa. He told me that I should probably get stitches, and that I would probably have another scar to add to the map of ruin across my forehead, cheeks, chin.

"No one can say you don't have a lot of character written all over your face," he said.

"Good thing you've still got your movie-star looks," I said, and pushed myself farther into him.

We stayed like that, pouring love back and forth while the rain landed outside, until night fell.

I eventually asked Ivan to turn the television on, with the sound down. Lying in the blue TV light, I was comforted by the sound of the rainfall and even the sirens outside. Ivan's face looked serene and beautiful in the muted light, and I took pleasure in watching it until I fell asleep in his arms.

The Big Fella

The next time I saw Ben, he was bigger and shaggier than ever, and he circled me just like before. The rays of his smile fell upon my heart, filling me with delight. We were on the banks of the Yarra, as before, though the river was thicker and muddier this time, after all the rains. He circled in close to get a look at my face, at the purple- and mustard-colored bruise surrounding my eye.

"Sexy," he said, then turned his head to look upriver, before turning back to look at me with a big gap-tooth smile, his unkempt lion's mane surrounding his head like sunshine. He seemed more shy this time, but really pleased to see me. I liked the attention. We stopped like that in the cool autumn breeze, sharing space, smiling, enjoying the sight of each other while breathing the same air.

I took it all in: his cigarette smell, the green leaves on the trees, the muddy river, the buskers, the shape of his smile, the size of his hands, the clouds swirling behind his head.

"So we going to go another round?" he asked, looking sheepish, turning his gaze toward the painted Prince's Bridge, purple in the evening light.

"Absolutely, champ," I said, feeling good, as though I was underwater.

"That's good," he said, looking me up and down. "Gee, you're an ugly fucker aren't you?"

"You can't even stand to look at me, can you?"

He laughed, his thick lips parting slowly as leaned his shaggy head down toward mine.

JULY 2002

Jameson Currier

I'm not convinced two men can have an honest relationship," I said. I had not said anything at all during dinner, remaining quiet and listening to the mix of political and sexual banter bounce between the other guests and our hosts, as Eric delivered one elaborately prepared dish after another to the table. My neighbors Eric and his lover Sean, a gay couple in their midfifties, threw little soirees biweekly in their Chelsea apartment for a combination of their single and coupled gay friends, in order to be matchmakers or therapists as the necessity of their friendships required. I was twenty-four that summer and staying in my older brother's apartment down the hall; it was often impossible to escape Eric's attentions as I came and went from the building, and I once amusingly accused him of installing a spy cam because he was so knowledgeable of my comings and goings—or lack thereof—particularly my desire for hibernating for long stretches on the sofa watching movie after movie, the titles of which he also seemed to know.

But it was my comment on the inadequacies of gay relationships that immediately stirred up my host that evening.

"Of course they can!" Eric answered me. "You've just had a bad experience." And then to his other guests: "Teddy is just talking nonsense. He's too young to really believe that."

"Think about it," I continued. "Two men. In a relationship. How much truth can there be?"

"As much as you can accept," Eric answered. "Not every relationship is the same. And sometimes just because a man has secrets, doesn't mean that he is not an honest man and truthful to his partner. Sometimes it's a matter of compromise, not truth."

"Maybe you just haven't met the right man," Sam said to me. Sam was a friend of a friend of Eric's. He worked in a foreign service program and had returned to the States and New York because of "family business," which none of us had asked him to elaborate on, respectfully considering it another off limit issue that evening. "Family business" could mean either a parent's illness or a sibling's marriage or divorce. Or it could be a deeper secret, a way to disguise one's own truth. Perhaps Sam had been in some kind of legal or financial trouble. Perhaps he was bisexual and married and had a child—or had fathered an illegitimate one. It was a mystery Sam was not ready to explain or reveal to anyone that evening.

But I was grateful that I didn't have to elaborate any further on my own disastrous personal experiences, and that the others around the dining table were now drawn into the conversation.

"Or perhaps you're too focused on sex being an equivalent of love," Sean said to me, jokingly. Sean was a psychiatrist, so everyone always gave his words more weight than those of his stockier partner, though Eric, a respected commercial photographer, relished being the foolish and more socially frivolous of the two. "I certainly had that problem when I was your age," Sean added. "Of course, I'm wiser now because my sex drive is not what it once was. But I don't think that sex should be the sole basis of a long-term relationship with another man. Too much disappointment."

"Are you saying I'm not sexy?" Eric whined across the table. "Or lousy in bed?"

This was followed by nervous laughter from everyone.

"Of course, as Eric said, every relationship is distinct," Sean added.

I was glad that the topic soon shifted back to Sam, who until recently had worked in Afghanistan, and as dinner progressed from drinks to salad to entrees to dessert, the tale of Sam's work in a clinic in the Bamiyan province unraveled as he recounted his experience aiding a television journalist who had been injured in an accident. The journalist was a mutual friend with Eric and Sean. And in the odd set of connections and circumstances of those at dinner that evening, the journalist who Sam had helped had once lived in my brother's apartment, before my brother had assumed the lease. Eric was particularly proud that he was able to join together all the pieces of this puzzle over a three-course meal.

I was tired that evening and after a rich and heavy dessert of Dutch apple pie and ice cream, I excused myself from the party and the other guests and went back to my apartment. I had found it increasingly difficult to be social with other guys, which Eric had noted, of course, and which had been the catalyst for the dinner invitation. That week I was also watching another neighbor's dog, Joe's black cocker spaniel named Inky, while Joe was away in Los Angeles. Inky was a beautiful dog, a princess who padded about softly and tossed her curly head and floppy ears at me; one of her unacknowledged blessings was that she pulled me in and out of the apartment so that I did not completely lose contact with the outside world. I was greeted with a whoosh of affection as I stepped through the apartment door, tiny paws landing just below the faded white of the knees of my jeans. I snapped on her leash and we went to the end of the hallway to wait for the building's sluggishly slow-arriving elevator.

As it finally arrived, Sam was leaving Eric and Sean's apartment, and I held the elevator door open while he said goodbye to the two men with handshakes and kissed cheeks. He joined me for the ride to the ground floor and Inky's brisk sprint through the lobby to the sidewalk.

I liked Sam. Unlike our hosts, who were forever filling empty spaces with nonsensical chatter and opinions, he was not much of a talker. He was a tall, handsome, masculine man, a guy's guy who always seemed to be well put together and admired, about three or four years older than I was, so I felt a more generational bonding with him than I had shared with our older hosts, who had, in the eleven months that I had lived in my brother's apartment, tried to step into the roles of mentor, parent or guide for me. There was also a quiet modesty to Sam, as evinced by the personal story he would not disclose at dinner—he had been as vague in many of his statements as I was that evening about my ruinous love life—and there had been no ounce of bravado when he had recounted his assistance of Eric's friend in Afghanistan. I admired the fact that he had boldly stepped into foreign service after graduating college, something I had not been able to do myself, and I envied him for having already amassed a handful of anecdotal adventures that he could recount to strangers over a meal. But it had also made me feel rather inconsequential in the fabric of gay life and that perhaps I had been wasting my life in the city. In the elevator I was bashfully shy—or rudely disinterested in him—but Sam gruffly complimented Inky's beauty and funneled me questions about her and her owner which kept both of us looking down at the curly black mop of her and not at each other.

It was a warm summer night in mid-July, and the day's heat still seemed trapped close to the sidewalk. I broke into a light sweat as I moved away from the air-conditioning of the building and into the city air. We walked silently together to the end of the block and were about to shake hands as we reached Eighth Avenue where Sam would head toward the subway stop to begin his journey back to Long Island.

On the street, a bike messenger—an Asian guy about our age in a tank top and bright green cycling shorts—suddenly rode across a pothole he had not seen in his path. He went flying over the handlebars and landed on the street, unconscious. From the angle where we were standing we had both witnessed the accident. The messenger had not been wearing a helmet for protection. Sam touched me on the shoulder as the guy was rising up in the air, over the handlebars of the bike and onto the pavement, as if to keep me in place and out of harm, and once the fellow had landed on the ground, Sam rushed into the street to aid him.

"Do you have a cell phone?" There was blood on his shirt from where he had leaned into the Asian boy's head to check his wound.

I did, but not with me. I stepped farther away from Sam and the accident and stopped another guy who was walking by and talking on a cell phone, and I tapped him on the shoulder and asked, "Could you call nine-one-one for us?"

He was a beefy sort of guy, wearing a formfitting T-shirt and carrying a shoulder bag, and I gathered he must have just been at one of the gyms that dotted the neighborhood. He nodded at me, hung up on his call, called the emergency line and explained to the operator where we were.

Before he had hung up, a police car arrived, followed by an ambulance, and soon the messenger was being lifted onto a stretcher.

I thanked the beefy guy, and he disappeared as Inky's restlessness tugged me to one end of the block and back so she could sniff around and do her business.

When the ambulance and officers left and the street was cleared of gawkers, it was just Sam and myself and the dog. Sam's clothes were soiled and his hands were caked with dried blood. The messenger would be all right—more blood and broken bones than serious internal damages, the medical workers seemed to think. His blackout had only been for a minute or so. But he was being taken to the hospital for stitches and further tests.

"You can't get on the subway like that," I said to Sam. "You can wash up and take one of my brother's shirts."

We walked back to the apartment building and self-consciously waited for the elevator. I tried to commend Sam on his quick actions, but it felt strained and awkward and I was tired and ready to be on my own for the night, and Inky was restlessly tugging at the leash because she knew she would soon get a treat when we were back in the apartment.

In the elevator I unhooked Inky's leash and she leapt down the hall when we reached my floor. Inside the apartment, I pointed to the bathroom—the layout was not much different from Eric and Sean's apartment—and went to give Inky a treat and then find a shirt for Sam to wear.

A few minutes later he emerged bare chested and asked if I had a plastic bag he could use to carry his soiled clothes back to Long Island. It was impossible not to take in his body's military athleticism—thick, muscled shoulders and arms and a nicely developed chest covered with black hair curving into a thin, dark line that traveled down the middle of his solid stomach and widened again above his navel. I handed him the shirt I had found in my brother's closet and went into the kitchen to find a bag.

Sam was in the living room wearing my brother's shirt when I handed him the plastic bag and, as he stuffed the soiled clothes inside it, he asked, "Do you think they were trying to set us up?"

"I know for a fact that they were trying to set us up."

He nodded and smiled and stepped a little closer to where I was standing.

"You're a nice guy," he complimented me. "It would be a shame to disappoint them."

I smiled and bowed my head, accepting the approval, and he kissed me on my forehead.

He was a big guy and it was a brotherly gesture, but it made me feel vulnerable. I lifted my eyes up to him, which was when his kiss fell against my lips.

Slowly, clumsily, as if being awakened from a deep sleep, I put my arms around his waist. His hands slipped around me and settled at the belt loops of my jeans, where he hooked his fingers as I moved my hands beneath his shirt and around to his chest. I had wanted to kiss him since I had met him at Eric and Sean's, and I held my lips open as he forcefully moved his tongue into my mouth, as if to prove that he had been interested in me, after all.

He tugged the bottom of my T-shirt and slid it up over my arms and tossed it behind him, and his hands moved to my waist as he pressed his mouth against the center of my chest. His lips rode up my neck, and I let him linger there till the pleasure was unbearable, and then I took the edges of his shirt and pulled them toward his head.

We stood bare chested now in front of each other, deep-tonguing and stroking each other's bodies. I rubbed his nipple between my thumb and forefinger while he moved a hand to my crotch and grasped the erection beneath my jeans. Then he unzipped my fly, pressed his hand inside and clutched my cock through the fabric of my underwear.

My hands moved to unbutton the top of his khaki pants and as the zipper gave way his trousers fell off his hips and puddled at his knees. He was wearing a pair of light blue boxers, tented from the head of his cock, and I reached my hand to his thigh and slipped my fingers under the hem of his boxers until I found its wide, mushroom-shaped head. His cock was warm and hard, and I clutched it and gave a few strokes, then found his testicles and cupped and squeezed them.

He pulled away from me as if to find his balance and breath, and I took the opportunity to slip out of my jeans. He sat on the arm of the couch and undid the laces of his shoes and stepped out of his trousers. He had a nice smile and I leaned over him and kissed him, and we fondled each other for another few moments, then I drew him up by his arms and he followed me into the bedroom.

We were rougher now, stroking, kissing, tweaking, nibbling. In the darkness of the bedroom I could see his smile, and he made soft noises of astonishment as we twisted and rolled around. I expected him to withdraw from my rising intensity, but he accepted it and pushed it farther. I wanted him to love me because I found him, in spite of whatever secrets he might possess, a good, honest man—and to love him in a way that could transcend the need for sex but would also embrace its deepest desires. I thought that if I could prove to him that I was a good sexual partner then he would also see that I could be a good boyfriend or husband for him, a mistake I continually made with every man I found my way into a bedroom with.

He asked if I had lube and condoms, and I rolled away from him and found them in the drawer of the nightstand. I thought he wanted to fuck me, but it was the opposite. I took it slow, fingering him till he was ready to accept my cock. He gasped and his chest flushed as I entered him, and I pulled out until he hungrily urged me back. He wanted to hold my neck as I fucked him, and I obliged until I realized I could curve my spine and take his cock in my mouth as I remained inside him. I felt entirely innocent and genuine with him, as if this were the first time I had ever done this with a guy and we were to do this together the rest of our lives. He was full of puffs of astonishment, and I could feel the muscles of his stomach clenching and shifting and I kept at him, unrelenting.

He pushed my lips away as his orgasm arrived, and I withdrew from him and finished myself off. I left him and toweled myself off in the bathroom, regarding the satisfaction of my smile and the raw, red patches on my shoulders and neck where his jaw stubble had burned my skin. Back at the bed, Sam toweled himself off, and there followed a long period of lying together cuddling, holding each other, rubbing our hands and fingers along skin and hair. I mentally reprimanded myself for pushing myself so emotionally into the sex and for stepping into what I really knew was to be another one-night stand. I knew it wouldn't go any farther with Sam than this pleasurable moment, and I felt the hurt and disappointment of it before he had even left the apartment.

"You must have been starved for affection there," I said, as I lifted myself out of his embrace, referring to his time working in Afghanistan.

"No," he answered. "Just the opposite. There was a local boy," he said, then quickly clarified, "...young man. He was a handsome young man."

He rolled over so that he looked out the window, away from me, and I followed him, wrapping my arms around his waist in an effort to keep us together. I could feel his voice vibrating through his skin and into my fingers as he talked. "It began innocently enough. Eye contact. Flirting. Holding hands."

"Holding hands?" I said and lightly laughed.

"Casually," he explained. "It's a gesture of friendship between men. Muslim men are openly affectionate toward each other in a way that would be regarded as odd—or gay—here, and it's easy to fall into their habits."

"I was working at the clinic," he said, after a pause, as if he had been reviewing a memory before he attempted to describe it. "Dispensing medicines at the makeshift pharmacy. Tending to walk-in emergencies. Trying to patch up all these problems with aspirin and Band-aids."

Now he laughed as I had, lightly, then continued. "The young boy showed up one day looking for work. I shooed him away because there was nothing for him to do but get in the way, and there was nothing to pay him with. But he returned about an hour later. He was really looking for food, and I gave him some bread and a chocolate bar I had saved since I was in Kabul. He was ecstatic. He knew a little English. They all know a little English there."

"Hello, Meesturh," Sam mimicked the accent. "I lihcke you. You lihcke me?"

We both laughed at the imitation, and Sam continued. "Like I said, it started with flirting. He was always smiling at me and he had a terrific smile—dimples on his left cheek you just wanted to drop your tongue into. He was always happy to help me with whatever I was doing. He made me smile. I gave him food every day. Bread I had taken from the guesthouse where I was staying and taking my meals. I would be grumpy in the mornings until he showed up, ravenous, and I watched him eat. He was sleeping in the caves up on the cliffs."

"The caves?"

"The grottoes on the hillside, carved by the Buddhist monks centuries ago. Where the ancient giant Buddhas had been. They were cold, nasty places, and I have no idea how he stayed warm at night, because it could get very cold. There were many families living in the caves, and I can only imagine that their body heat was what was warming them—when they had food to fill their stomachs. The boy had been separated from his parents at a refugee camp, and he was staying with his older sister's family—her husband and a little baby girl. He wouldn't eat all the food that I gave him. There was always something that he tucked away in his pocket that I knew he would give to one of them later. It was heartbreaking if you stopped to think of it, but there was so much to think about, that this was only one minor thing. Every day there was another casualty or a patient with a problem—an abscessed tooth or a broken toe. *Something*. It was such a cold, harsh place. Beautiful. But *hard*."

He continued. "One night I was able to bring him to the guesthouse to dine. It was owned by a local Muslim man and his wife, and they had always objected to my suggestion of him eating with us, in spite of my offer to pay extra to have the boy there, then one night they changed their mind. He ate with us—the rest of the MSF staff in the clinic and a few of the Red Cross guys who were also in the house—and they all knew him and were glad to have him with us. He helped the owner carry out the dishes of food and clean up—we ate on the floor, sitting on pillows and using our hands most of the time. There were three or four of us staying in each of the rooms, and instead of having the boy walk back in the freezing dark to the cliffs I had him sleep beside me on the floor. It was a simple, polite gesture. I was just trying to be a good Samaritan, but I knew it would create trouble for me one day. He stayed with me every night after that. Each night he slept closer and closer until we were sleeping together. It was just so natural. One day I knew I was in love with him."

"This was the fellow who drove the van?" I asked. "To the hospital. To Kabul?"

"Yes," Sam said. His body was tense, frozen into thought.

"How old was he?"

"I don't know."

Then again, after a pause, he added, "It was part of why I left. He was too young. I wasn't sure what I could give him. So I ran away."

"You ran away?"

"I left him in Kabul. I told him that I had to return to America for a while, because of a family problem; that I would be back soon. He took it okay, because I convinced him that I was coming back. There was no family problem."

"Are you going to go back?"

"I've gotten a new assignment. Working in Tunisia."

He lay still for a while, breathing slowly in and out. Then we both rose and showered together, stroking each other to another orgasm beneath the warm flow of water.

Clean, exhausted and back in the bed, I drifted off to sleep in his embrace. I sensed him stir hours later, rise out of bed and begin to get dressed. The activity aroused Inky in the other room, and I groggily stayed awake until Sam was dressed and at the door.

"Good-bye and thanks," he said, as he left. "I hope you find him."

I nodded and closed the door, petting Inky and groping my way through the darkness of the apartment and back to sleep. I was by then too tired to miss him, but I knew I would in the days that followed.

HOW BOYS FLIRT WITH OTHER BOYS

Eric Nguyen

Senior prom tastes like salt. It's because seventeen-, eighteen- and nineteen-year-olds sprawl on wooden floors not made for dancing. Not that anybody's dancing, not much anyway. Even though this is the last dance of the year, everyone acts like it's freshman year all over again.

Geeks like Billy Lee—dark eyed, with darker framed glasses—stand against the walls, wondering why they came. He came with a girl, a girl with blonde hair, even though her last name is Chan. There are no blondes in this town. Except her. And now she's halfway across the room, her hands on some girl, and Billy feels like going home and telling his mom that Laura Chan is a dyke. And that she likes black girls.

Laura Chan would probably get angry, though. As far as Billy knows, she's always angry. And she'd tell Mrs. Lee, "Well, Billy's a fag too. He's been eyeing that Bobby all night."

Billy imagines the scene in his head as it unfolds, and in it he says, *His name's not Bobby, it's Robert, and he likes being called Robby, not Bobby, and I couldn't help but eye him, he plays basketball and baseball, and he wrestles too, and he stayed behind one year, but we're practically the same age; at some points during this year we were even both eighteen.*

Everyone knows Billy's a fag already except for his mom. But the cool thing is that everyone's okay with it, for the most part. Okay means they don't talk about it. They smirk and call him "different" in a tone that everyone gets. Everyone has always treated him this way. Everyone except Robby.

Robby comes up to Billy and asks him how prom's going.

"So-so," he says. He leans harder into the wall. He wonders, *If I lean back far enough, would the wall fall over?* But what he's really thinking about is holding Robby's hand and walking around the prom like that and then maybe dancing. *The nerve*, he thinks. It's what daydreams are made of. He's thought about it for all four years they've known each other. Walking to class with Robby, Billy thought about letting his hand touch Robby's, maybe slightly, but he stopped himself. Yet this was the only reason Billy chose the same classes as Robby. Even shop. Thinking back on it, he realizes he could have cut a finger off, and then who would want to hold his hand? *Love makes you a dummy, even puppy love*, Billy thinks.

Robby says, "Yeah, sorry about Laura. She's such a dyke." They both laugh. "She so dykey!" says Robby in his best imitation of how Asians are supposed to talk. He watches Margaret Cho too much, and she's funny because they've never seen Asians talk that way before. Not even Billy's mother.

"Yeah," Billy says and waits because there's always that awkward silence that he can never get used to, even with Robby. "How's your date?" Billy means Cynthia, who played on the lacrosse team, varsity with the blue shirts, Number 5.

"Cindy's over there," Robby says, pointing across the room

to a redhead giggling among brunettes. Her hair made her some type of commodity in town. It made her different, but her white skin made her the same, so she was safe to approach and destined for whatever popularity a high school could afford.

"And it's only nine," says Robby.

"I can never get used to dances. Not even prom." Prom was supposed to be important, Billy thought. But without someone—anyone but Laura Chan—it all seems useless, like any other day. Blaring pop music—Lady Gaga on repeat—he could have done this in his room, in his boxers. Heck, he could've done it naked. "I need air," he says.

"I'll come," Robby says.

Across from the school, there's a playground with fake wood chips and a jungle gym colored like a rainbow. Billy says that he doesn't know why they built it in the first place because it's not like anyone comes out here. "No one plays on playgrounds anymore. And why near a high school?"

"So kids like us can have one more chance at childhood. Before whatever comes next." Robby hangs on the monkey bars and the last syllable of *whatever comes next* hangs between a question mark and an ellipsis. He's a whole two inches above the ground. "What does come next?" he asks.

"There's a college. In Maine."

"Maine?" Robby says.

"Yeah, Maine. What're you doing?"

"I don't know, staying here, I guess. Community college, I think."

"That's good," Billy says. He knows lots of kids going to community college, staying in town, and maybe things will never change for them. At eighteen he knows this for sure: things never *do* change here. His mom works at the cereal-packing plant, she's been there all his life. His sister puts on too much makeup and spends too much time in front of the mirror, even though the same people always show up at the bar where she works, and she can't even get on full time. And his father—who knows what happened to him? Mrs. Lee says he ran away with a gypsy, and Billy thinks of Natalie Wood on TCM. But Maine is something: a fresh beginning, a new journey, far away from here. He is partially excited.

"What you gonna do in Maine? Is that where people like you go?" Robby laughs sarcastically, as if questioning Billy's choice of Maine—of all places!

"No one goes to Maine to be gay," chuckles Billy. "Stop being stupid!"

"You're being stupid," Robby says, "Going so far away." Robby lets go of the monkey bars and drops onto the ground, his good dress shoes cracking the fake wood chips. They scratch his shoes, so he sits on a metal donkey, the kind that you bounce on, and takes them off. Billy follows, riding a donkey beside Robby, even though he's too big for it. They're both too big, more men now than boys.

"They're my dad's shoes," Robby says and wipes one of them with his hand and then the sleeve of his shirt.

Billy smiles.

"What you smiling at, Billy? Keeping something from me?"

He wants to tell Robby that he's smiling because out here is so much better than in there. Because in there someone keeps requesting the same Lady Gaga song, and it's too dark to really see anyone or anything, and the disco balls make him dizzy anyway, and Laura is on that other girl and everyone thinks it's okay, it's almost hot, and there he was, alone against a cold wall that he wished would crumble if only he leaned hard enough. If only he leaned hard enough, then maybe all the school's walls would crumble and he could run away with Robby, because Robby is the closest he's ever had to a best friend, mainly because he never asked him, *How did you get that way?* Or said, *You're a freak, you know, you're a walking, talking, breathing freak.*

He even got into the habit of calling himself a freak in the morning, as he brushed his teeth and combed his hair.

Robby didn't say those things, though. Robby was cool. Robby actually sat down with Billy at lunch, at the loser end of the cafeteria where one lightbulb is always out, and that one lightbulb makes all the difference.

"Nothing," is all Billy says. "I'm not smiling at anything."

Robby drops the shoes and bounces some on the metal donkey. It makes a rusted sound like the door of an old house. *He's like a kid, definitely like a kid*, thinks Billy. He begins to bounce too, as if competing to make noise.

A car passes by slowly; there are two signs at the corner, one displaying running children, another that reads PROCEED WITH CAUTION. The two boys stay silent as the car rolls straight on through, as if they're afraid someone will find them.

"Can I ask you a question?" says Robby.

"You already did."

"Mind if I smoke?"

They both pause: because they forgot that it's okay to smoke at their age, because they still wanted to know that someone was there to give them the "okay" or the "go ahead."

"Go ahead," Billy says.

Robby takes a fresh pack from his back pocket. He tears it open at the dotted line and points it at Billy.

"Nah," Billy says. And that's the last that is said for another while.

* * *

From his donkey perch, Billy watches students leaving and reentering the school, boys running from girls, girls chasing boys, because that's how girls flirt; it's in the chase.

How do boys flirt? Billy asks himself. *How do boys flirt with other boys?* He wonders now, again, about asking Robby, because that's what best friends are for, advice. And Billy's always giving advice about girls to Robby—give them lotion, the pink kind, call her back, don't wait!—as if he knew more about girls than Robby, even though he never notices them. They're like wallpaper, he wanted to say, they're there because they *are*, even though you don't know what for. He wonders how it would sound to ask Robby about flirting. Flirting has to be the same for everyone. But Billy's hands are sweaty, as the boys sit, together and alone, in the dark, and he's waiting for something to happen, anything to happen, anything at all. He hears screaming, joyful screaming, and the sound of high heels on asphalt. "Give me that back!"

He thinks, maybe boys steal each other's shoes and chase each other around and squeak and squeal like girls. Or maybe it's all done with notes on last week's homework, accompanied by a smile from across the room, as if smiles were a secret language. Or possibly they meet in abandoned playgrounds at night, smoking and riding metal donkeys while everyone else is busy someplace else, with someone else.

The one time Robby gave him a note was during seventh period, asking to meet him near the basketball courts after school. There he showed Billy how to roll a joint and smoke it without inhaling it too deeply into his lungs. They got so high they thought they were going to die, or else their parents would kill them, for coming home smelling like dope. So they hid out in Robby's van the entire night with the sunroof open, counting stars and making wishes. "I wish I were I rich man," Robby had said. "I wish…" Billy had said. He coughed on purpose to stall. The hot and humid space smelled like salty sweat and armpits, and on the radio Nirvana sang "Smells Like Teen Spirit." Nirvana, because jocks listen to Nirvana, not Madonna.

"Kurt Cobain died on my birthday, you know," Billy had said.

"Of course I know that, you already told me that," Robby had said. He had rolled over and they were face-to-face in the back of a van. "Tell me something I don't know," he had said, so close that his breath brushed Billy's cheek and the smell of the weed, the weed that made them think about death, tickled his nose. They thought often about dying.

"I don't know," Billy had said, and laughed. Recalling that one time, now, Billy thought he had laughed. It seemed like a laughing moment. *He should have laughed.*

"I'll tell you something you don't know," Robby had said, leaning in closer, as if this was going to be a secret, licking his lips as if it'd be the last thing he'd ever say….

That was when a teacher banged on the window and told them to go home and clean up, after confiscating their dollar-store lighter and rolling papers. That was their moment, a secret story to tell each other that starts with, *Remember when…*

And that was why, for the rest of the school year, Robby smiled at him from across the room, a grinning smile with his teeth biting his lips to hold in the laughter, but they both ended up chuckling anyway.

Hearing the laughter over at the school, boys' deep voices chuckling and girls' high-pitched voices giggling, Billy thinks back to that moment and wonders what the answer is, what it is that he doesn't know about Robby. He conjures a list in his head, ranking what he really wants last, because everyone knows you never get to the bottom of lists: Robby once robbed a bank with a ski mask, he ran into the building, telling everyone to get down on the ground *or else;* Robby's favorite hobby is knitting, but he only does it on Sundays and only when it's raining because that's when he's bored; when Robby was twelve he killed a squirrel with a BB gun, the squirrel's name was Pussy, and that's why he can't have sex with the pretty girls: because he can only think of Pussy; and: Robby likes me—he really, really likes me.

Billy stops thinking when smooth, wet skin touches his cheek. Lips, he guesses. But it's not a peck. The lips stay for a long second before the tender suction lets go.

Billy's heart hiccups in his ears, and he knows his face is turning red. And Robby says quietly that he has something to tell Billy, something he's been meaning to tell him for a long while.

"I have stuff to tell you," is what he says.

"What kind of stuff?" Billy says.

"All kinds of stuff," Robby says, bashfully, breathing through his mouth, baring his teeth—a kid who doesn't know what to say, a kid whose hands are shaking, a kid whose eyes are twinkling with tears. He falls back on the metal donkey and drops his cigarette onto the fake wood chips or maybe his shoes, who cares, no one notices, because Robby kinda smiles, kinda doesn't and then says, "This is when I knew..." and sighing smoke into the air and starting again, "This is when I first knew..."

Senior prom tastes like salt and smoke and Robby.

ABOUT THE AUTHORS

JAMESON CURRIER is the author of two novels, *Where the Rainbow Ends* and *The Wolf at the Door*, and four collections of short stories, *Dancing on the Moon; Desire, Lust, Passion, Sex; Still Dancing* and *The Haunted Heart and Other Tales.* "July 2002" is an excerpt from his new novel, *The Third Buddha.*

MARTIN DELACROIX (martindelacroix.wordpress.com) writes novels, novellas and short fiction. His stories have appeared in more than a dozen erotic anthologies, and he has published two novellas, *Maui* and *Love Quest.* He lives on a barrier island on Florida's Gulf Coast.

SHANNA GERMAIN (shannagermain.com) plays chess like a queen but falls in love like a pawn. Her writings on lust, love and leviathans have appeared in *Absinthe Literary Review*, *Best American Erotica*, *Best Gay Bondage*, *Best Gay Erotica*, *Best Gay Romance*, *Best Lesbian Erotica*, *Best Lesbian Romance*, *Dirty Girls* and more.

DERRICK DELLA GIORGIA (derrickdellagiorgia.com) was born in Italy and currently lives between Manhattan and Rome. His work has been published in several anthologies and literary magazines.

DAVID HOLLY's stories have appeared in *Best Gay Romance, Best Gay Erotica*, *Surfer Boys, Boy Crazy* and many other publications. Readers will find a complete bibliography at gaywriter.org.

TYLER KEEVIL grew up in Vancouver, Canada, and moved to Wales in 2003. Since then, his work has appeared in a variety of magazines and anthologies, including *Front & Centre*, *Interzone*, *New Welsh Review* and *On Spec*. His first novel is titled *Fireball*.

JAY MANDAL comes from southern England. He has written three novels: *The Dandelion Clock*, *Precipice* and *All About Sex*; and three collections: *A Different Kind of Love*, *The Loss of Innocence* and *Slubberdegullion*. He also has a collection of short stories and another of flash fiction awaiting publication.

DAVID MAY (bydavidmay@comcast.net) is a Hawaiian national living in Seattle with his husband and two cats. He is author of two fiction collections, *Madrugada* and *Butch Bottom & the Absent Daddy*; a collection of nonfiction, *A Nice Boy from a Good Family* and an advice column, "Cum What May," for M4Mkink.com.

ANTHONY MCDONALD lives in England. His stories have appeared in many anthologies, and he is the author of three novels: *Adam, Blue Sky Adam* (also available on Kindle) and *Orange Bitter, Orange Sweet.*

TOM MENDICINO spent six raucous years eking out a living in the sales departments of several New York publishing houses before attending the University of North Carolina law school. Since 1994, he has practiced as a health-care lawyer; his debut novel is titled *Probation.*

EDWARD MORENO has finally settled down in Melbourne after years of wandering aimlessly in search of pleasure. A native of New Mexico and a one-time San Franciscan, he now calls Australia home. He studies writing and Spanish at the University of Melbourne. His work has been published in *Best Gay Erotica* and at blithe.com.

ERIC NGUYEN (youfightlikeannerice.blogspot.com) is a writer from Maryland.

SIMON SHEPPARD (simonsheppard.com) edited the Lambda Award–winning *Homosex: Sixty Years of Gay Erotica* and *Leathermen;* wrote *In Deep: Erotic Stories; Kinkorama; Sex Parties 101; Hotter Than Hell* and *Sodomy!* and has been published in more than three hundred anthologies.

ABOUT THE EDITOR

RICHARD LABONTÉ dropped out of university in 1970 to work for a daily newspaper in Ottawa, Ontario, left professional journalism in 1979 when his then-lover asked him to help open the first branch of A Different Light Bookstore in Los Angeles, and left bookselling (and San Francisco) in 2000 when the then-three bookstores, in West Hollywood, New York City, and SF were sold to new owners. He returned to Canada in 2001, imported his husband Asa in 2003 (Canada: legal marriage!), and this century has worked as a freelance editor and book reviewer, cobbling together more than thirty anthologies for Cleis Press and Arsenal Pulp Press and syndicating a queer book review column, "Book Marks," for a decade. Bowen Island, British Columbia, rural population more or less 3,500, is now his home, where he's happy to see more deer than people most days of the week.